HOW THE BIG PRIG GOT HIS SHIRT UNSTUFFED BY THE COXEMAN

Lord Brice-Bennington was so repressed that he was a threat to the safety of the Free World.

Rod Damon—the Coxeman—had to make a swinger out of him or he'd never be able to get the information on a scandal that could explode and topple the British government.

How does he do it?

Well, he uses every trick he ever learned (and taught) in the League for Sexual Dynamics.

What kind of tricks?

Satisfy your curiosity at once.

The tale begins in Chapter One. . . .

COXEMAN #11

IT'S WHAT'S UP FRONT THAT COUNTS

AN ADULT NOVEL BY BY TROY CONWAY

POPULAR LIBRARY

Copyright © 1969 by Coronet Communication, Inc.
All rights reserved. Except as permitted under the U.S. Copyright Act of 1976, no part of this publication may be reproduced, distributed, or transmitted in any form or by any means, or stored in a database or retrieval system, without the prior written permission of the publisher.

Popular Library
Hachette Book Group USA
237 Park Avenue
New York, NY 10017

Popular Library is an imprint of Grand Central Publishing. The Popular Library name and logo is a trademark of Hachette Book Group USA, Inc. The Coxeman name and logo is a trademark of Hachette Book Group USA, Inc.

Visit our Web site at www.HachetteBookGroupUSA.com

First Printing: March 1969

Printed in the United States of America

Conway, Troy
It's What's Up Front That Counts / Troy Conway
(Coxeman, #11)

ISBN 0-446-54316-0 / 978-0-446-54316-3

CHAPTER ONE

It began—where else?—in bed.

It began with a bazoomy bundle of bombastic energy whose name I never learned and whose face I never got to see because the lights were already off when I got to the party.

The party? More precisely, the annual office party of the League for Sexual Dynamics.

The League—or L.S.D., as it used to be called before a certain hallucinogenic drug gave the initials a bad name—is a legitimate research organization of which I am the founder and director.

I, of course, am Dr. Rod Damon, the man who brought the personal touch to the field of sex research—or, as I'm better known among readers of these books, The Coxeman, reluctant superspy for the United States Government.

For the benefit of those of you who don't know about my past exploits, I'll provide a brief biographical sketch a few paragraphs hence. But first let me tell you about the party.

The annual office party of the League for Sexual Dynamics is a sextravanganza to end all sextravaganzas. Its purpose, purely and simply, is to serve as an escape valve. Despite the incredible amount of sexual stimulation which we at the League experience in the course of our work, we make it a point to keep a tight rein on intra-office passions. We naturally participate in sex acts with our subjects, and we naturally have our own private sex lives. But, because we realize that there's a point beyond which you can't safely mix business and pleasure, we keep away from each other—three hundred and sixty-four days a year.

The three hundred and sixty-fifth day—appropriately enough, Havelock Ellis' birthday—is the day we let loose. From six p.m. on September fifteenth to six p.m. on September sixteenth, we stage a nonstop, twenty-four-hour, intra-office orgy.

Every staff member and employee of the League comes to

5

the orgy with a date who can be counted on to swing along with the best of us. After dinner, drinks and a round of stag movies, the lights go out and we play musical beds.

Each of the females present is assigned to one of the cubicles in the League's subterranean laboratory. Each cubicle is equipped with a cot, a liquor cabinet and a variety of sexual appliances. The cubicle occupied by the League's senior female researcher—a delectable brunette with a Ph.D. in abnormal psych and a body that'd make Wilhelm Reich want to take a flying leap out of his orgone box, by name Angela Lee—is also equipped with an alarm clock, the bell of which can be heard throughout the laboratory.

When the girls are in place, the guys pick numbers from a hat to determine who goes to which cubicle. Once everybody has been paired off, the action begins—and continues for exactly one half hour. Then the alarm clock in Angela Lee's cubicle goes off, and each guy moves down the line to the next cubicle.

This sexual round-robin continues, interrupted only by brief pauses for food and drink, until exhaustion retires the participants or until the six p.m. curfew rolls around. In the interests of preserving everyone's anonymity—so as to avoid repercussions during the three hundred and sixty-four days until the next party—the lights never go back on while the guests are coupled off. Consequently, the guys never get to see the girls they're playing the game with, and the girls never get to see the guys.

When my date and I arrived at the party, the lights had already gone out. We'd gotten tied up in traffic, and we missed dinner and the stag films. But we arrived in time for the drawing of numbers from the hat. While Angela Lee hustled my date off to an empty cubicle, I took my place at the tail end of the line of guys who were drawing numbers.

I drew cubicle number nine, where I found the bazoomy beauty mentioned earlier. Evidently not a person given to wasting time with amenities, she had already stripped to the altogether and was sitting expectantly on the edge of the cot. I felt my way to her, my hands zeroing in instinctively on her full, ripe breasts. She reciprocated by gripping me at the groin before I even had a chance to sit down on the cot next to her.

Her mind evidently was unprepared for what her hands found. "Wow!" she beamed, obviously both surprised and pleased. "You're ready already! This is going to be quite some night."

6

I was inclined to agree with her. It doesn't take much to turn me on, but, even if it did, this doll could've done the job. The feel of her creamy-smooth breasts set off a spark inside me, and the provocative caresses with which she was favoring my genitalia fanned the spark into rapid flame.

Without releasing her grip on me, she stood and offered me her mouth. Then, as my tongue probed its moist sweetness, she unzipped my fly.

Her slim, cool fingers played expertly against the hot, rock-hard pillar of my manhood. She fondled it lovingly and appreciatively, much like an artist might fondle an especially fine piece of sculpture. Standing on tiptoe and arching her body toward me, she nibbled teasingly at my lips. At the same time, she began rubbing the blunt end of my instrument against her belly.

I started to unbutton my jacket. "No," she whispered, "don't take your clothes off. I want to undress you."

Obediently I let go of the jacket, and, reaching behind her, started stroking the firm, soft flesh of her inner thighs. They quivered in response to my touch, and, pressing her body harder against me, she parted them slightly to give me easy access to the well of passion which lay at their juncture. I took the cue, and found that the well was far from dry.

"Mmmmmmmmmm," she purred as my fingers invaded her nether-lips, "that feels good." Pause. "*Very*, very good."

What she was doing to me felt very good too. And what she did next felt even better.

Ever so slowly, she eased her body away from mine and lowered herself to her knees. On the way down, she paused long enough to take my manhood between her breasts and rotate them tantalizingly against it. Then her breasts weren't there anymore and her face was. She pressed my eager engine against her cheeks, covered it from bottom to top with a torrent of moist, tantalizing kisses and finally hid it deeply between her pursed lips.

I caressed her silky smooth hair, which was soft and straight and shoulder-long. The guy-wires of my passion were as taut as violin strings. Her mouth was hot and marvelously tight around me, and every movement of her talented jaws sent new waves of excitement coarsing through me. My hips fell automatically into a slow, thrusting rhythm. The warm glow in my gut told me that relief couldn't be more than a swallow away.

But she wasn't about to let the game end that quickly. Sensing that I was very close to the point of no return, she abandoned her maddeningly arousing jaw movements and began playing against the sides of my shaft with her tongue and teeth. The technique made me tremble with excitement. But the hotter I got, the farther away my boiling point seemed to be. No doubt about it, this chick knew her stuff!

She also knew, or seemed to, that I wanted to make love to her in the good, old-fashioned way. And she evidently shared my feelings. Still tonguing me like a clarinet player gone ga-ga over a new mouthpiece, she undid my belt and eased my trousers down my legs. I stepped out of them, and she tossed them aside. Then, replacing the tongue action with some more mouth action, she gently removed my shoes and socks.

I shucked off my jacket and unloosened the knot on my tie. She had said that she wanted to undress me, but I was too eager for the main course to waste any more time with aperitifs. She evidently understood my urgency, because she didn't protest.

I had my tie, shirt and T-shirt off quicker than you can say "Masters and Johnson." Then, clutching her under the arms, I lifted her to her feet. For a moment we just stood there, then, hugging and kissing like a pair of sex machines gone wild, we tumbled onto the cot in a tangle of arms and legs. A few seconds later, her legs scissored open and I, like the Durango Kid leapfrogging onto his horse, lunged into the saddle.

Ordinarily I'm not much of a guy for quickies. My stamina is one of my key stocks in trade. I'm a long-distance runner who can run with the best of them.

But this doll's foreplay had been enough to wear down even my resistance. By biting on my lip and concentrating on the pain to take my mind off what was happening down below, I managed to hold off for about a minute and a half. Then the volcano erupted, and my lava bubbled over inside her.

Fortunately her sexual responses were as quick as mine. No sooner had I gone off than her fingernails tore into my back and her hips began moving frantically. The spasm that shook her body told me that she had climaxed along with me. My reputation as a man who never flies solo remained intact.

For a minute or two afterward, we just lay together in the silence of delicious mutual exhaustion. Then she suddenly noticed something.

"You . . . you . . " She paused, as if trying to think of a delicate way to say it, then blurted out, "You're still up!"

I kissed her playfully on the lips. "Yep. Are you ready for another round?"

She was bewildered. "But . . . I mean . . . I *did* please you, didn't I? . . . I mean . . . you *did* come . . . didn't you?"

"I sure did! I came and now I'm back again." I was grinning because I still remembered how good it felt.

"But . . . I mean . . . you're still *up!* I mean . . . how can that be? Unless . . . unless . . ." Recognition suddenly dawned on her. "You're Doctor Damon!" she declared. "Wow! You're Doctor Damon!"

(An aside to the reader who is meeting me for the first time in these pages and is unaware of the reason she recognized me: one of the reasons I've been so successful as a sex researcher is that I'm an extremely virile male. As a matter of fact, I'm insatiably virile. For as long as I can remember, I've been afflicted—or, if you prefer, blessed—with a condition called "priapism." In every case other than mine known to medical science, priapists experience perpetual penile erection but are unable to achieve orgasm. Thanks to an unexplainable biological quirk, I'm different: I enjoy the best of both worlds; I'm not only always rarin' to go, but I inevitably have one hell of a time when I get there. My delicate companion evidently had heard about my condition. Word of mouth is the best advertising there is.)

I acknowledged that I was in fact Doctor Damon. She favored me with another appreciative "Wow!" Then her voice took on a worried tone. "Gee," she said, "my boyfriend'll kill me if he ever finds out I asked you your name. I mean, he said that nobody was supposed to ask anybody their names here. He said it was all supposed to be anonymous. He said there was a rule. But I heard about your insatiable virility . . . and . . . and . . ."

I cut off her sentence by kissing her, then said, "Don't worry about a thing. You didn't ask me my name, you told me. And I'm not going to tell anyone you did."

"I mean," she continued, obviously not reassured, "I've heard so much about you. . . . And I always wanted to meet you. . . . I mean, what girl wouldn't want to make it with the world's foremost authority on sex? . . . And . . . and . . ."

I kissed her again. "Then let's stop talking about it and let's make it again."

"Okay. . . ." She sighed her relief. "I mean . . . well, what I mean is . . . well, *okay!*"

We made it again. It took us a lot longer this time. In fact, it took us the rest of our allotted half-hour. The alarm clock in Angela Lee's cubicle went off just as I was having my second climax and my ever-more-enthusiastic partner was having her fifth. Reluctantly I severed our union, kissed her goodbye and moved on to the next cubicle, clothes in hand. En route I cursed myself for establishing the rule about anonymity at the League's annual office party. This was one doll that I woud've liked to have seen again—and again—and again.

I felt my way around the new cubicle. The cot was empty, and so was the chair next to it. "Yoo hoo," I called, "anybody home?"

Suddenly a flashlight flicked on from the wall alongside the door. Its beam landed on my face. "Damon?" asked a female voice.

"Hey," I replied, "no lights allowed. And how did you know my name?"

"I'm from The Coxe Foundation," said the voice. The flashlight flicked off.

I swallowed hard. My first reaction had been surprise. My second was anger. But both the surprise and the anger quickly gave way to resignation. I'd been playing the Coxeman game for too long now to expect that there was anything I could do other than say "yes" when I was called on for another mission. And I obviously was being called on. I never heard from The Coxe Foundation unless I was.

"Damn," I murmured futilely, "not again."

"Again," said the voice. The tone suggested that its owner was enjoying my displeasure.

I grunted. "You could at least have waited until tomorrow. I'm used to being interrupted by you bastards at the oddest moments, but the night of the League's annual office party—that's downright nasty."

"We had to move quickly," came the reply. "Every minute lost puts the Communists a step closer to getting the B-bomb and taking over England."

"What B-bomb? And when in hell did the Communists get involved in England?"

"You'll get all the details soon enough. Now come with me." She reached out and took my hand. "We've wasted too much time already."

I followed her out of the cubicle and through the corridor to the laboratory's rear door. She seemed to know the place as well as I did. I wondered how she had become familiar with the layout, and how she had gotten in in the first place. All the entrances had been locked, and only the invited guests had keys.

She opened the door and gestured with her flashlight toward the stairs which led to the main floor of the building. I preceded her up them. "How come they sent you for me?" I asked. "What happened to my friend with the walrus moustache? Usually he does his own dirty work."

"He's indisposed," she said softly.

"Something serious, I hope? Like leprosy, maybe?"

She didn't bother to answer that one.

At the top of the stairs, she gestured with her flashlight for me to open the door and we stepped outside. In the greenish-white glow of the lights over the doorway, I finally got a look at her. Her face was more than vaguely familiar. I was positive I had seen it before, though I couldn't be certain when or where.

But one thing I *was* certain of: she was one of the prettiest girls I'd ever seen. Her eyes were shaped like a cat's—wide on the flanks and in the middle, then narrowing to a sharp point on the insides. Her nose was smallish and straight, and her jaw was a perfect oval. Her mouth was wide and its corners were turned slightly upward, as if she were perpetually about to break into a big, warm smile. Her hair was honey-blonde and parted in the middle; it tumbled around both sides of her face, as though it couldn't stand being so close to something so beautiful without touching it.

And her body was nothing to sneeze at either. That's an understatement. I've come across a lot of sensational shapes in my time, and this one could hold its own with the best of them.

She was about five-five and probably not more than a hundred and ten pounds. And her breasts were two generous portions of pleasure. She wasn't wearing a bra, but they were young and firm—deliciously tempting. Her blouse was a see-through, and my eyes searched hard for the pinkness of her areolae. Unfortunately the light wasn't bright enough.

She stood facing me and waited until my eyes had done their tour of duty. Then, when they met hers, she said acidly, "Do you like what you see, you filthy sex maniac?"

I did a double-take. I'd been called a sex maniac before, but never by a doll who bounced around sporting a pair of un-corseted thirty-eight-C's under a see-through blouse. "Yes, I like what I see," I said. "But what's this 'sex-maniac' routine?"

11

She gave me a dirty look. "I know all about you, Damon. You're a pervert and a despoiler of innocent women, and your books poison the minds of helpless children all over the world. I may be forced to work with you on this mission, but that doesn't mean I can't still hold you in utter contempt."

"Holy Moses," I wheezed, unable to think of anything else to say.

She gave me another few seconds of her withering gaze, then turned and started down the narrow path leading to the sidewalk. Walking behind her, I got a good look at her flip-side. It was every bit as inspiring as the what's-up-front that the cigarette ads tell you is supposed to be what counts. Her buttocks—ungirdled, naturally—were big and firm, just like her breasts. They alternately rose and sank in cadence as she walked, and my imagination conjured up all sorts of delightful little games to play with them.

I decided to try warming up to her—in my own weird way. "Uh, look, whatever your name is," I fumbled, "I don't know what charm school you went to, but didn't they ever teach you that you can catch more flies with sugar than with vinegar?"

"I'm not interested in catching flies," she deadpanned.

I still couldn't believe that a doll who looked and dressed like she did would hold me in contempt for being a devotee of sex. "Uh, this may sound like a line," I said, taking another stab at warming her up, "but I'm sure I've seen you somewhere before."

"You're right," she replied tonelessly.

"Where did we meet?"

"We didn't. What you're right about is that it does sound like a line."

"But I have seen you. I'm sure of it."

"Well, I've never seen you before in my life. And it would suit me fine if I never saw you again."

By this time we were at the curb. She gestured with her flashlight toward a parked Volkswagen. I got in the passenger side. She walked around to the driver's side, slipped in behind the wheel, kicked over the ignition and pulled into traffic.

"Uh, look," I said, making one last stab, "you might hold me in utter contempt, but that doesn't mean we can't still be friends, does it?"

"It does in my books," she said, not taking her eyes from the road.

That ended our conversation, and as we rode along in

12

silence, I permitted myself to entertain a few nasty reflections about The Coxe Foundation, about its present emissary, about the man with the walrus-like moustache who seemed to be the brains behind the organization, about life in general, and especially about a very-mature-looking sixteen-year-old who was, in a way, the main reason The Coxe Foundation had its hooks into me.

Until a few years ago, if anyone had told me I would one day risk life and limb playing spy games with America's enemies, I'd've laughed in his face. I was very comfortably ensconced in my position as associate professor of sociology at one of the major universities in the northeastern United States, and I got all the kicks I needed from my work with the League for Sexual Dynamics.

The League was something I had cooked up in my predoctoral days when I was a sex-happy young student trying to figure out a way to both have my sociological cake and eat it too. I applied for grants from knowledge-hungry foundations and used the money to study the sexual mores of various segments of contemporary society. My findings were published in all the major journals, earning me a reputation as one of the country's most distinguished behavioral scientists, and my field studies led to my bedding down with some of the grooviest chicks ever hatched.

My first project had been a study of the sexual behavior of American coeds, my next a study of parallels between the sexual behavior of American coeds and contemporary non-college females. Subsequently, I had studied the sexual behavior of female grad students, of female Ph.D.'s, of female college dropouts, of female college kick-outs, of suburban housewives, of urban housewives, of rural housewives, of New York career girls, of Los Angeles career girls, of London career girls, of Paris career girls and of Rome career girls.

Somewhere along the line, my studies must have come to the attention of the Thaddeus X. Coxe foundation, an ostensibly right-wing front-group for the United States' most secret espionage agency. One night while I was playing research games with one of my students, I was interrupted by two hoods from this agency. They took me to the boss, an elderly man with a shaggy, walrus-like moustache and a W.C. Fields sense of humor and whose name I never was able to learn and whom I thereafter referred to simply as Walrus-moustache.

Walrus-moustache had learned of a plot by a group of Neo-Nazis based in Hamburg, Germany, to lure the United States,

13

Russia and China into World War III. He also had learned of the aforementioned very-mature-looking sixteen-year-old, who had participated in one of my early research projects. Since carnal knowledge of a person younger than eighteen is, in my state, statutory rape, punishable by twenty years imprisonment, I had two choices: (1) Go to jail, or (2) become a Coxeman and spy on the Neo-Nazis. I chose to become a Coxeman and stopped the war before it ever got started.

I was sure I had dispatched all of Uncle Sam's enemies once and for all, but I was wrong. No sooner had I returned to the university and settled down with my work than Walrus-moustache found another Coxeman caper for me. Then another and another, ad nauseum. Now, evidently, I was being tapped for another mission—and unless I wanted to have those statutory rape charges brought against me, I had no choice but to go along. Cursing my fate, I slid down in the seat of the Volks and stared blankly out the front window.

After navigating through the traffic on Campus Avenue, my unfriendly chauffeuse wheeled onto the main highway. Less than a mile later, we passed a moving van which was parked at the side of the road. The lights on the Volks blinked, and the van lights blinked in reply. Then the van lumbered onto the highway behind us.

Slowing to a crawl, the Volks pulled to the right of the highway and let the van pass. A moment later the back doors of the van slid open and a ramp was lowered for the car to enter the van. Then the doors closed and my companion ushered me down a narrow corridor to a tiny office located up front near the cab.

My friend with the walrus moustache was seated behind a desk which occupied a good fifty percent of the office's floorspace. When he saw me, he stood, smiled engagingly and thrust out his hand. "Damon, my boy," he beamed, "how nice of you to drop in! Long time no see, as the saying goes."

"Stash it," I growled, "What's the pitch this time?"

His face took on an expression of sincere hurt. "Ah, Damon, after all we've been through together, you're still hostile. What a pity, because I genuinely like you. Do you suppose your hostility has deep psychological roots? Perhaps your mother toilet-trained you improperly? Have you thought of consulting a psychotherapist?"

"I'll tell you why I'm hostile," I said angrily, "and it has nothing to do with toilet training. Tonight in the middle of a

14

very private affair you sent this underdressed ice cube"—I looked around for my escort, only to find that she had left—"you sent this broad who says she holds me in utter contempt because I'm a sex researcher——"

"Ah," he smiled, "you mean Miss Randall."

I stopped short. I had wondered where I'd seen the ice cube before, and now I knew. She was Robbi Randall, the starlet whom all the Hollywood columnists were touting as a sure thing to become the screen's number one sexbomb!

She came into the public eye with a big, resounding *wham!* when she appeared completely nude in a Broadway play. Then she appeared completely nude in three low-budget movies, the last of which depicted her engaging in coitus with two men, at more or less the same time. Now, according to the newspapers, she had been signed for a big-budget film to be made by a major studio. And when she bared her charms in *that* one, she was sure to be well on the way to superstardom.

"Robbi Randall!" I whistled under my breath. "How did you get your hooks into *her!* And where the hell does a broad like that come off saying I'm a despoiler of innocent women?"

Walrus-moustache smiled. "Miss Randall is a method actress."

"Marlon Brando is also a method actor, but he never told me that my books poison the minds of helpless children all over the world! And *he* never balled two girls on screen in full Technicolor nudity! Robbi Randall is a first class hypocrite—and she has a lot of nerve to boot!"

Walrus-moustache's smile broadened. "Miss Randall is merely playing a role she feels compelled to play under the present circumstances. When the mission is over, you'll probably find that our female Coxeman is as eager to hop into bed with you as you are to hop into bed with her."

My eyes widened. "Female Coxeman?"

"The first. Sit down," he said, taking a bottle of Johnnie Walker Black from a nearby liquor cabinet and pouring me a stiff drink. "I'll tell you all about it."

Actually, sitting down was the last thing in the world I wanted to do, but I remembered those statutory rape charges which still could be brought against me. And, frankly, I remembered what Robbi Randall had looked like with her unholstered thirty-eights poking out at me through the sheer

15

fabric of her sexy see-through. So she was the first female Coxeman in the history of the Foundation, was she? And she'd be eager to hop into bed with me when the mission was over, would she?

"Okay, tell me," I said, grinning. Taking a healthy swallow of Johnnie Walker Black, I sat down.

CHAPTER TWO

"Damon," said Walrus-moustache gravely as he peered at me over the top of his desk, "the nation is in serious trouble. Unless The Coxe Foundation acts quickly, the enemies of freedom may acquire a weapon more terrifying than the A-bomb, more terrifying than the H-bomb, indeed more terrifying than any weapon now known to man. Moreover, even if they don't acquire it, they can do irreparable damage to America's cause. As things now stand, the sun may be about to set on the British Empire. Every minute lost puts the Communists a step closer to taking over England. If that happens, of course, the world balance of power will shift against the United States—perhaps for all time."

He poured himself a drink and held it up to the light, as if examining it for foreign particles. "First let's talk about the Communists." He sipped the drink. "You probably didn't know they were on the move in England, did you?"

"I never really thought about it," I admitted.

"Well, apparently neither did anyone else until one of The Coxe Foundation agents uncovered a little stunt that seems to be their doing. Do you remember the Profumo scandal of 1963?"

"Who doesn't?"

"Two very highly placed Members of Parliament evidently don't. If they do, they seem not to have learned a lesson from it. They've taken up where Profumo left off."

I grinned. "You mean Christine Keeler has come out of retirement?"

His wince told me what he thought of my sense of humor.

16

Continuing as if I hadn't interrupted, he said, "One of the M.P.'s is Christopher Smythe. You may have heard of him. He's the fellow who's always making those vituperative anti-Russian speeches in the House of Commons that get so much play in the right-wing press over here. The other is James Whelan. He's in the House of Lords and is pretty much unknown on this side of the Atlantic, but his reputation as a Russophobe is strong in England and on the Continent. Both of these gentlemen are married and the fathers of children. Yet, both are carrying on shamelessly with London playgirls of the lowest level. Smythe's friend is a Soho hooker named Andi Gleason. She used to be a performer in one of those private clubs where the evening's entertainment includes girls making love on stage with snakes, among other disgusting doings. Whelan's girlfriend is another prostitute, by name Diane Dionne. She's never made it publicly with a snake, so far as I know, but she's done just about everything else, and she's reportedly very heavily involved in London's underground drug scene."

He paused, as if to make sure that everything he'd said had sunk in. I nodded to acknowledge that it had, but my expression also let him know that I didn't see what the big deal was. "So two married men have shady ladies on the side," I said. "It's been known to happen before."

"Yes, and when it happened to John Profumo the reverberations almost toppled Prime Minister MacMillan's government. What do you suppose would happen now—in the face of the devaluation of the pound, and all the other problems the British have been having—if a scandal broke involving Smythe and Whelan, two men who play a far more crucial role in Prime Minister Wilson's government than Profumo played in Prime Minister MacMillan's?"

"Wilson's regime would be in trouble?" I replied, playing the straight man.

"To put it mildly. More likely than not, Wilson would have to seek a vote of confidence. And if he did, his government might fall. Even if it didn't, the scandal still could be catastrophic for the United States. You see, Smythe and Whelan are two of the best friends we have in Parliament. Time after time they've advanced our cause when most other M.P.'s were against us. Without them on our side, England would not be nearly so willing to see things our way when international disputes arise."

He took another sip of his drink. "Now," he continued,

"both Smythe and Whelan are up for reelection. They're being opposed by candidates whose views are much more to Russia's liking. One candidate is an avowed anti-American, and the other is a middle-of-the-roader who has taken occasional anti-American stands. If these candidates win, we're in genuine trouble. And if a scandal breaks involving Smythe and Whelan, these candidates almost certainly will win. As you can see, it's quite a problem."

"Maybe I'm obtuse," I said, "but I don't see the problem at all. If we're so concerned about a scandal, why don't we just call Smythe and Whelan aside and ask them to lay off their girlfriends—at least until after the election?"

His sad smile told me that he deemed me something of a novice about international politics and the *modus operandi* of the Coxe Foundation. "We did ask them to lay off. We approached them on a very high diplomatic level and pleaded with them to walk the straight and narrow. Despite the fact that we presented them with irrefutable evidence that they're carrying on, they flatly denied all charges and told us to buzz off."

"I don't get it. If our evidence was irrefutable, how could they deny the charges?"

He took a packet of snapshots from his jacket pocket and tossed them to me. "Here's the evidence. Judge for yourself if it's irrefutable."

I examined the photos. There were ten in all. The first four showed a lean, silver-haired man engaged in a variety of sexual gymnastics with a tall, leggy blonde. The next four showed a paunchy guy in his fifties playing sadie-massie games with a hefty but pretty brunette. The last two were newsmagazine headshots of Smythe and Whelan, included presumably for comparison purposes.

"Well?" Walrus-moustache prodded. "Is there any doubt in your mind that the men with the girls are Smythe and Whelan?"

"They could be just look-alikes," I reminded him. "Or the photos could have been doctored."

"Out of the question. The agent who took these pictures is one of our most trusted men. He tailed both Smythe and Whelan to the apartments where the pictures were taken, and he tailed them home afterwards. We have no reason to believe that he'd lie to us. In fact, the only reason he took the photos was so we could show them to Smythe and Whelan as proof

18

positive that we knew what they were up to."

"And they still denied the charges?"

"Yes. They claimed that the men in the photos had to be look-alikes—even though we knew this wasn't the case. That's one of the reasons we think the Communists are behind this whole thing."

"You just lost me on the clubhouse turn. How does their denial suggest Communist involvement?"

He took another sip of his drink, then leaned back in his chair. "Through the years that we've been dealing with them, Smythe and Whelan have shown themselves to be eminently astute and pragmatic politicians. It's virtually unthinkable that either of them would jeopardize his career just because he's taken a fancy to a pretty girl. We can only conclude that they somehow or other have lost control of their actions. Perhaps drugs are involved, or perhaps there's been some subtle form of brainwashing employed. In any case, Smythe and Whelan seem to be hooked on the girls—so hooked that they won't attempt to extricate themselves, even though their careers and their lives will be ruined if a scandal breaks."

"That still doesn't mean that the Communists are involved."

"True, but all indications point that way. This sort of entrapment tactic is very definitely a part of the Communist espionage network's way of doing things. Also, both playgirls, Andi Gleason and Diane Dionne, have been seen in the company of a man whom we know to be one of Russia's top British spies—a double-agent, in fact, who hasn't reported a word of the Smythe and Whelan business to his superiors in Her Majesty's Secret Service. Conceivably it's all a fantastic coincidence. But I doubt it. From where I sit, the whole deal looks like a Commie operation from start to finish."

I polished off my Johnnie Walker Black and handed him my glass for a refill. "Okay," I said, "suppose it is a Commie operation. Suppose the Reds did use Andi Gleason and Diane Dionne to get Smythe and Whelan hooked. If the Communists are really behind this thing, they've had at least as good a chance of photographing Smythe and Whelan *flagrante delicto* as The Coxe Foundation had. And if they've got the photos, they can set off a scandal any time they please. What can we do at this point to stop them?"

He handed me a fresh drink. "Not much, I'm afraid. We're compelled to conclude that if the Communists do have the

19

photos, which we may assume they do, they don't plan to use them to help Smythe and Whelan's opponents win the election."

My eyebrows arched quizzically. "What else could they use them for?"

"Well, one possibility is that they plan to blackmail Smythe and Whelan into doing their bidding after being returned to office. Remember, the elections are less than two months away. If the Communists have the photos, why haven't they used them already? It can't be just a case of waiting for the opportune moment. The sooner you break a scandal like this, the better off you are. If the Communists waited until a few days before the election, the only people who'd really be hurt would be Smythe and Whelan. If they broke the scandal now, they could insure the defeat of dozens of other anti-Communist M.P.'s who've been allied with Smythe and Whelan in the past—and perhaps even the fall of Prime Minister Wilson's government."

"But," I objected, "are Smythe and Whelan so important in Parliament that the Communists would pass up a chance at toppling Wilson's government just so they could blackmail Smythe and Whelan into playing the Commie game once they get back into office? It doesn't make sense."

"No," he acknowledged, "it doesn't—which is why we suspect that the Commies may be playing for bigger stakes."

"Bigger stakes? Like what?"

"The B-bomb." His eyes fixed to mine. "Honestly, Damon, the prospects of the Communists getting their hands on it make me shiver in trepidation." He drained his drink, shuddered, and poured himself a fresh one.

"Just for the record," I put in, "what in hell is the B-bomb?"

He took a sip of the new drink. "Does the phrase, 'C.B.R. warfare,' mean anything to you?"

"Of course. Every ex-soldier knows it. Chemical, Biological and Radiological warfare."

"Precisely. So far—fortunately for the world—the major powers seem to have forgotten about the 'C' and the 'B.' They've concentrated only on the 'R,' or radiological, aspect. But unfortunately some minor powers have begun to investigate the 'C' and the 'B' and a year ago a certain minor power—which for security reasons we'll refer to henceforth as Country X—developed a bomb which, in its own way, is far more fearsome than the atom bomb, the hydrogen bomb and all the other bombs in the radiological warfare arsenal. Because its action is biological, we call it the B-bomb."

"What exactly does it do?"

"It contaminates vegetable growth. Unlike conventional bombs, it doesn't detonate on contact with the earth. Rather, it is exploded in the atmosphere, at an altitude of between forty thousand and sixty thousand feet above sea level. Its particles then spread out over a radius of a thousand miles. Some fall directly to the earth, while others are absorbed by clouds and fall to the earth as part of a rainstorm or snowstorm. In any case, within twenty-four hours after the bomb has been released, all vegetable growth within a thousand miles of the release-point is contaminated. And since the particles are microscopic, there's really no way of knowing that the bomb has been released until after the target area begins to suffer the ill effects. By then, of course, it's too late."

I shrugged. "So people eat contaminated vegetables. Is that so bad?"

"It's nothing less than disastrous. The contamination, you see, doesn't merely involve the spreading of infectious viruses or bacteria. Rather, it involves the implantation of pathogens which, when consumed by humans, disrupt the D.N.A. chains in the body's cells. You know what D.N.A. chains are, I assume."

"Vaguely. They have something to do with the transference of genetic characteristics, don't they?"

"Yes, but they also play a key role in the cell's synthesis of protein. If the cells fail to synthesize protein, they no longer are able to sustain themselves."

"In other words, everyone in the contaminated area dies?"

"Yes, but it's a slow and most horrible death. The brain cells, which are the most complex, go first, and the people in the contaminated area become walking zombies—unable to think clearly, unable to control their actions, unable to function on any rational level. There is neither law nor order; the world of the contaminated becomes literally a mad world, a world which is an insane asylum with no caretakers. Next, the cells of the stomach, the liver and other vital organs are affected. The result is general bodily decay. Like lepers, the victims begin literally to rot away. Finally the heart cells go, and the body dies—if the victims haven't all committed suicide or killed each other first."

His face ashen as he contemplated the picture he had painted, he took a healthy swallow of Johnnie Walker Black. "Now, Damon, I repeat: one B-bomb can contaminate an

21

area with a radius of one thousand miles; ten B-bombs, strategically dropped, could contaminate the entire United States and much of Canada and Central America. If our enemies had these bombs and chose to drop them on us, we'd have no way of knowing that we were under attack until we were already on our way to a mass grave." His eyes found mine. "The prospects are disquieting, wouldn't you say?"

I nodded. "You're a master of understatement."

He sipped his drink. "Fortunately, Country X, which developed the B-bomb, is a neutral nation which generally leans toward the West. Once the bomb had been developed, the President of Country X contacted the chiefs of state of the United States and England. He offered to share the bomb with us if we shared our A-bomb and H-bomb with him. We, of course, couldn't do so without violating existing treaties with the other atomic powers. But we did persuade him to accept another arrangement. Under this arrangement, the United States and England pledged that they would place their atomic weaponry at Country X's disposal if ever Country X was attacked by another nation. Country X, in turn, agreed to disband its biological warfare laboratory and destroy the formula for the B-bomb."

I whistled under my breath. "Our diplomats must have really worked overtime to sell *that* proposition."

He smiled. "That's why they call diplomats diplomats. In any case, Country X went along with the deal. The United States and England then appointed a six-member committee, composed of three Americans and three Britishers, to supervise the disbanding of the biological warfare laboratory. The Americans on the commission included a high-ranking member of the Senate Foreign Relations Committee, a very highly placed Undersecretary of State and a prominent governor whose parents had migrated to the United States from Country X. The Britishers included a VIP from the Home Office and two M.P.'s, one from the House of Commons, the other from the House of Lords. The M.P.'s, as chance would have it, were Smythe and Whelan."

I put two and two together and came up with a very disconcerting four. "In other words, you think that the Communists are holding off on exposing Smythe and Whelan's hanky-panky because they think Smythe and Whelan have the formula for the B-bomb?"

"Not quite. Actually, we're pretty certain that Smythe and Whelan don't have the formula. But, in supervising the disbanding of the biological warfare laboratory, they couldn't help but learn something about the bomb and the people who developed it. Evidently Russia is interested in finding out precisely what—and whom—they know. In this sort of operation, the tiniest scrap of information can be invaluable. For example, if either Smythe or Whelan reveals the names of the scientists who were involved in developing the bomb—names which both Smythe and Whelan, along with the other four members of the inspection committee, certainly know—Russia might abduct one or more of these scientists and force them to share their findings with Russian scientists. Anything that Smythe or Whelan might reveal can put the Russians a step closer to developing a B-bomb of their own, which is why we believe the Russians are resisting the obviously-very-strong temptation to set off a scandal which might topple Prime Minister Wilson's regime."

"But," I reminded him, "you don't know for sure that the Russians are aware of Smythe and Whelan's hanky-panky. And you don't know for sure that the Russians are aware that Smythe and Whelan were members of the committee that supervised the disbanding of Country X's laboratory. As a matter of fact, you don't seem to have a shred of evidence that Russia even knows Country X developed the B-bomb. You're piling assumptions on top of assumptions, but there are no facts beneath the assumptions; it's all guesswork on your part."

He smiled. "The espionage game, Damon, is ninety-nine percent guesswork. What separates the winners from the losers is who guesses best."

"All right, let's say that your guesses are all on target. What can the United States do at this stage of the game to keep Smythe and Whelan from spilling whatever beans they have to spill?"

His smile broadened. "We might arrange to have them assassinated."

I gulped. "You wouldn't."

He sighed. "You're right, we wouldn't. Even though the enemy doesn't abide by the Marquis of Queensbury's rules, we do. I don't have to tell you that this makes The Coxe Foundation's job a lot harder than it has to be." He sipped his drink. "But the job is still there to be done, so we've got to figure out another way of doing it. Right now, I think, our best move is to separate Smythe and Whelan from their girlfriends. That's where you enter the picture."

"Me?" I gulped again. "If your diplomatic sources couldn't persuade Smythe and Whelan to stop seeing the girls, I certainly won't be able to."

"No, but you might be able to persuade the girls to stop seeing Smythe and Whelan."

"How in hell am I supposed to do that?"

"That's your problem. But I think you can solve it. After all, Damon, your abilities as a lover are legendary. And there's nothing that can turn a girl's head like love."

"You mean you want me to make Andi Gleason and Diane Dionne fall in love with me? And then you want me to talk them into breaking off with Smythe and Whelan?"

He looked at me like a schoolteacher looks at a particularly bright pupil who has just answered a very difficult question. "That's precisely what I mean. I want you to go to London and really win these girls over. You'll have an unlimited expense account, as usual, and you'll get whatever other support from us that you ask for. Use what we give you, along with your own natural talents, to convince Andi and Diane that they can't live without you. Then figure out some way to get them on a plane out of England as soon as you possibly can. I don't want them anywhere near the British Isles until after the election is over."

"What's the point in that?"

"Well, as things now stand, the girls seem to be the Russians' only link with Smythe and Whelan. If the link is broken, the Russians won't find out anything more about the B-bomb until they forge another link. While they're trying to forge it, our side will have more time to work on Smythe and Whelan and, hopefully, bring them back in line."

"Maybe," I suggested, "they won't try to forge another link. Maybe they'll just give up on the B-bomb and use their photos of Smythe and Whelan's hanky-panky to set off a scandal."

He shook his head. "In my experience, the Russians don't operate that way. They never settle for the consolation prize when there's still a chance at copping the grand prize. Besides, even if they did try to set off a scandal, chances are they wouldn't suceed if Andi and Diane weren't around to back their play."

"I don't follow you."

"Well, think about it for a moment. Photos, as you've observed earlier, can be doctored. If the Communists do have photos—which we can assume they do—they could turn them over to Smythe and Whelan's opponents. But if the opponents level charges at Smythe and Whelan, the charges can always be denied. And, if Andi and Diane aren't around to offer personal testimony, Smythe and Whelan just might be able to persuade their constituents that the charges are trumped up. Picture, if you will, one of these opponents claiming that Smythe or Whelan is a poor security risk because of his involvement with a girlfriend. When asked for proof of involvement, he produces the photos. But, of course, no newspaper could ever print them, and even if the photos were circulated privately, no one could be positive that they hadn't been doctored. At this point, Smythe and Whelan challenge their opponents to produce the girls with whom the alleged affairs were carried on. The girls can't be produced, because they simply aren't around. Perhap a few witnesses will say that they saw Smythe and Whelan with the girls. But witnesses, as everyone knows, can be bought—and the only witnesses anyone can really come up with are friends of Andi and Diane, prostitutes and pimps whose credibility is certainly open to question. Without Andi and Diane, the charges fall, and Smythe and Whelan escape unscathed." He looked to me for agreement.

"It works nicely in theory," I said. "But how about in practice? If you had to bet a million dollars one way or the other, would you put your money on Smythe and Whelan?"

"The bet, I'll admit, would be something less than a lead-pipe cinch. But the strategy I've outlined seems to be our only practical move at this point. The odds against us are formidable, but we've got to buck them, because they're the best odds we can get."

I leaned back in my seat and let everything he had said sink into my brain. The more I thought about the whole business, the more formidable the odds seemed.

If I did succeed in getting Andi and Diane out of England, there was no guarantee that the Communists wouldn't find out what they wanted to know about the B-bomb anyway. They could always use two more girls to play Mata Hari with Smythe and Whelan once Andi and Diane were gone.

If the Communists did find out what they wanted to know about the B-bomb, there was no guarantee that they wouldn't still use their information about Smythe and Whelan's extra-curricular activities to set off a scandal which might topple Prime Minister Wilson's government. They could set off a scandal afterwards just as easily as they could before—even more easily, in fact, because they would then have proof positive that Smythe and Whelan were abominable security risks.

Meanwhile, if they didn't find out what they wanted to know about the B-bomb, they could still set off a scandal any time they chose. If Andi and Diane weren't around to testify against Smythe and Whelan, the new girls certainly would be. I couldn't just keep on luring away playmates forever.

Actually there was really no guarantee that I'd even be able to get close enough to Andi and Diane to make my love-magic work on them. If they were Commie stooges, as Walrus-moustache believed, they'd be damned suspicious of any American who tried to get within a hundred yards of them.

For that matter, if the Commies ever spotted an American trying to get within a hundred yards, they might very well decide to put that American out of commission permanently—with a bullet in the head.

"How," I asked Walrus-moustache, "do I keep the Commies from suspecting what I'm up to?"

His smile told me that he had anticipated the question. "We've got that all worked out for you, Damon. We've set you up with the perfect cover, a cover which the Commies wouldn't suspect in a million years. Your friend at court in this caper will be none other than Lady Brice-Bennington."

I did a double-take. "Lady-Who?"

"Lady Brice-Bennington. You've heard of her, I trust."

"You mean the famous bluenose?"

"Yes, the famous bluenose. Our code name for her is 'The Big Prig'."

My double-take became a triple-take. "You're damned right I've heard of her. And if she's going to be my friend at court, I've got a funny feeling that I'm not going to need any enemies at court."

"Don't be too sure. What do you know about her?"

"Well, for one thing, she thinks sex is the greatest evil in the world. She wants to do away with all erotic books, all sex scenes in movies and all government-subsidized sex research. She's organized a group of do-gooders called the Friends of Decency, and they're putting pressure on Parliament to pass the most stringent laws against fornication, adultery, homosexuality and other forms of nonmarital sexual indulgence since Emperor Constantine held sway in Rome."

"What else do you know about her?"

"Her Friends of Decency tried like hell to keep my books

26

from being circulated in England and they almost succeeded. Eight publishers were cajoled into refusing to print my last sexual survey before a ninth finally decided to take his chances with it. And *that* poor bastard almost went out of business when he did. The Friends of Decency persuaded more than five hundred English bookstores not to handle any title he published."

"Okay, what else do you know about her?"

"Not much, other than the fact that she hopes eventually to desex the whole damned British Empire."

"Then let me fill you in on a few details. For one, she's a staunch supporter of Smythe and Whelan's opponents. Smythe and Whelan, you see, are very much in favor of relaxing Britain's censorship laws. In fact, two years ago, Smythe in the House of Commons and Whelan in the House of Lords introduced bills which would abolish completely the British Censorship Office. The bills didn't pass, thanks mainly to lobbying by Lady Brice-Bennington's Friends of Decency. But the Big Prig didn't content herself with that small victory. She vowed that she would get Smythe and Whelan turned out of office, and she's been working steadfastly ever since to make good her vow."

"And *that* makes her *my* friend at court?"

"No. But Robbi Randall does."

It was time for another double-take. "You'd better explain," I said.

"I shall." He smiled. "When The Coxe Foundation first learned that Smythe and Whelan were flirting with a Profumo-like scandal, we had no reason to suspect that the Communists were involved. So we asked ourselves who would benefit most if Smythe and Whelan were turned out of office. One of the first names that came to mind was that of The Big Prig. We subsequently assigned agents to follow Andi Gleason and Diane Dionne twenty-four hours a day, and we learned something which we found very interesting. Over the space of two weeks, one highly placed member of The Big Prig's Friends of Decency made no fewer than three visits to the Soho strip-joint where Andi Gleason had worked before she became a full-time prostitute. During the same period of two weeks, another highly placed member of the Friends of Decency attended several pot parties at which Diane Dionne was present. While these revelations didn't necessarily prove that the Friends were scheming to set Smythe and Whelan up for a Profumo-like scandal, we felt that we should investigate

27

the Friends a little more thoroughly than we had in the past. Accordingly, we assigned our female Coxeman, Robbi Randall, to infiltrate the organization and tell us something about its inner workings."

"Robbi Randall? The Lady Godiva of stage and screen? How the hell could *she* persuade a bluenose like Lady Brice-Bennington to even let her in the same room, let alone infiltrate the Friends?"

"To answer that question I'll have to tell you a little bit more about Lady Brice-Bennington. Apparently one of the things you don't know about her is that, before she became The Big Prig she was pretty much of a playgirl herself. To be sure, she wasn't in the same league as Christine Keeler and Mandy Rice-Davies. I doubt that she ever went to bed with a man for money. But she's had more than a fair share of non-paying lovers. In fact, she once was known as the Prone Joan of Shaftesbury Avenue."

"Amazing."

"Not really. Scratch a sexual reformer and you often find a former playboy or playgirl. That was true of Mary Magdalen, St. Paul and St. Augustine in Biblical times, it was true of Caesar Augustus and Emperor Constantine in Ancient Rome, and I suspect, though I must admit the evidence is far from irrefutable, that it was true of Queen Victoria and Prime Minister Gladstone in nineteenth-century England. On this side of the Atlantic, there has been——"

"Okay, okay," I interrupted, "you've made your point: The Big Prig sowed a few wild oats before her nose turned blue. That still doesn't explain how Robbi Randall was able to infiltrate the Friends of Decency."

"Elementary, my dear Damon. If there's anything a repentant sinner thrives on it's the recognition of another repentant sinner. All Robbi Randall had to do was present herself to Lady Brice-Bennington, express remorse about the shameful use to which she had permitted her body to be put on stage and in films, and say that she had seen the light. She was welcomed with, to coin a phrase, open arms."

"She must have done one hell of an acting job," I commented.

"She did. But then, I knew she would. Despite the sensational nature of her film and stage roles thus far, she's a fine actress, fully deserving of the Oscar which I'm sure she one day will win."

"Okay, save the press-agentry. I'll take your word that she's another Sarah Bernhardt. Now explain why she cold-shouldered me tonight."

He chuckled. "Well, as I said before, she's a method actress. Method actresses don't merely play a part, they live it. Robbi presently is living the part of a Friend of Decency."

"Does she have to live it twenty-four hours a day—at home as well as abroad?"

"Some actresses are more methody than others. But if you really want a sample of what she's like when she steps out of character, I'll give you one."

My smile was more of a smirk. "You're damn straight I want a sample!" I enthused.

He pressed a button on his desk, and a buzzer sounded somewhere outside. A few seconds later, Robbi Randall came in.

I looked.

And I looked again.

And because I still could hardly believe my bulging eyes, I looked a third time.

I had, of course, got a glimpse of Robbi outside the laboratory of the League for Sexual Dynamics and in the Volkswagen on the way to our rendezvous with the van. But the light had been too dim for me to really see very much.

I also had seen her on the screen. But the wonders of modern cinematic technology notwithstanding, a photographic image is never quite the same as the real thing.

Now, in Walrus-moustache's brightly lit mobile field office, I was seeing the real thing—Robbi Randall in the flesh. And I mean *in the flesh!*

Her see-through blouse was a see-through to end all see-throughs. It concealed absolutely nothing. Her marvelous breasts jutted out through the gauze-thin cloth in all their canteloupian splendor. The nipples were big, blood-red and proudly upthrust. They gave way gently to the soft-pink hues of her silver-dollar-sized areolae—two glorious oases of color set against fields of pure alabaster-white, And her breasts really were white; the Albino-fair flesh was untinged by even a ray of sunlight.

Beneath these enormous and perfectly shaped ornaments, her belly was smooth and flat. Her skirt hung low on her hips, and I was able to perceive the exquisite concavities and convexities where her hips and abdomen joined. Unfortunately, I couldn't view the totality of torso-limb juncture; mini though her miniskirt was, it still was a skirt and not a G-string. But I

29

saw enough to let my imagination fill in what was missing. And what I imagined would have been enough to raise my standard if priapism hadn't already raised it for me.

The bottom of her miniskirt fell just a silly millimeter or two below the underslope of her buttocks. Then came her marvelous legs—slender but very shapely, strikingly white and flecked beautifully with tiny blonde strands of soft, short hair. The effect was breathtaking.

And then there was her face—that perfect face, with the catlike eyes, the tiny nose, the superb jaw and the unbelievably exciting mouth that always seemed ready to break into a big, warm smile. Such—to paraphrase a fellow writer of considerably greater literary renown—is the stuff wet dreams are made on.

Robbi tossed me a quick dirty look as she entered the room, then stood in front of Walrus-moustache's desk. She regarded him with an expression of such docility and obedience that I wouldn't have been surprised if she said, "Sir, you rang?"

"Robbi," he told her in a friendly but authoritative voice, "Damon has to be convinced of your acting ability before he leaves for England with you, so I'm going to ask you to let me direct you in a brief improvisational scene."

She was looking at him with the intensity of a person who has been hypnotized. Her singularity of focus was so great that she appeared not to have even heard his reference to me. She said nothing and waited for him to continue.

"The character you're going to play," he went on, 'is a twenty-three-year-old girl named Ellen. She's married to a middle-aged invalid named Max, who hasn't made love to her since their honeymoon, when he was injured in an automobile accident and became paralyzed from the waist down. She never really loved Max anyway, and married him only because her parents forced her into it. Her real love has always been Jean-Claude, whom she met at a Swiss ski resort when she was nineteen, and for whom she has hungered insatiably ever since."

I watched her face as he spelled out the circumstances of the character she was going to play. Subtly—at times, almost imperceptibly—changes came over the beautiful face. She already was getting into the part. Her eyes, her mouth, even her cheeks seemed to me to be the eyes, mouth and cheeks of the unhappy young housewife Walrus-moustache was describing.

"Twice after her marriage," he continued, "Ellen met Jean-Claude. The first time was at Geneva, where she had accompanied Max on a visit to a famous neurological clinic. The second time was in New York, where Jean-Claude had come to be interviewed on a TV sports show. Both times Ellen and Jean-Claude made love, and the experience was for her the most glorious experience in her life."

On cue, Robbie's expression became one of near-ecstasy, as if she were mentally reliving the two boudoir episodes of Walrus-moustache's implausible scenario.

"Then," continued The Coxe Foundation's answer to Elia Kazan, "tragedy struck. You read, Ellen, that Jean-Claude was killed in an avalanche in the Pyrenees, where he was competing in the midwinter olympics. You were heartbroken. Life lost all meaning to you."

Her face quickly reflected heartbreak and the meaningless of life.

"Then," said Walrus-moustache, his voice becoming more animated, "you received a phone call ten months later from a physician who was a friend of both you and Jean-Claude and who knew about your affair. I am that physician. When I phoned you, I told you that Jean-Claude was not dead—that, in fact, he was right here in my office, waiting to see you. I asked you to come here as quickly as you possibly could."

These new circumstances, like the ones which preceded them, were reflected with incredible believability in her face.

"Now I want you to go outside and take a minute or two to put yourself in the mood for the scene where you will greet Jean-Claude, who will be sitting on the couch here"—he gestured toward me—"when you arrive at my office. Your dominant condition before you enter the office will be one of expectancy and yet disbelief; you will have no reason to think that I lied to you, and yet you will be unable to bring yourself to accept that Jean-Claude actually is alive. Then, when you enter the office, you'll see Jean-Claude. The memories of all your wonderful times together will flash through your mind, and you'll be overcome with emotion. You'll throw your arms around him, kiss him, and then, because the scene *is* improvisational, you'll respond in whatever way you think you should." He permitted himself a small smile. "Do you have any questions?"

"No," she replied quietly.

"Fine. Then step outside, get into character and come back in to play the scene whenever you're ready."

Not looking at me, she left the room. Walrus-moustache favored me with a grin. "Well, old buddy, here's your big chance. Just remember that her name is Ellen and try like a bastard to get into the character of a Tristan about to be reunited with his Isolde."

"Gotcha, C.B.," I quipped, eager as all hell to get the show on the road. Actually I'd never considered myself much of an actor, method or otherwise, but I was sure that once I had my arms around Robbi Randall's sensational superstructure I'd play a Jean-Claude that would put John Gielgud's Hamlet to shame.

A minute passed, then another. I sat hunched over on the couch and tried to think the sort of thoughts I imagined Jean-Claude would think. Unfortunately all I could think of was how badly I wanted to give Robbi Randall a dose of the medicine I'm best at dishing out—which didn't impress me as a very Jean-Claudian thought. But what the hell, even if my performance was lousy I'd still have had a crack at the sex bomb of the seventies who suddenly had become Number One on my Most Wanted Persons list. That was enough for now.

A third minute passed, then a fourth. Then the door opened, and Robbi stepped hesitantly into the room.

She glanced at Walrus-moustache, who nodded in my direction. Then she wheeled toward me.

I stood. "Ellen!" I murmured hoarsely.

For an instant she was motionless. Her eyes were wide with incredulity, as if she were face-to-face with a ghost. Then, lips quivering, she ran toward me. Her eyes suddenly were brimming with tears. "Jean-Claude!" she gasped. Then, sobbing ecstatically: "Oh, Jean-Claude, Jean-Claude, Jean-Claude!"

My arms closed around her waist, pulling her body against mine. Her breasts heaved passionately against my chest, and her pelvis pressed hungrily against my manhood. She buried her face in the nape of my neck. I could feel her tears, hot and sticky, against my flesh. "Jean-Claude!" she moaned. "Oh, Jean-Claude!"

Evidently my potential acting talent was greater than I had expected it would be, because, all of a sudden, I found myself believing I actually was Jean-Claude. "Ellen!" I whispered urgently, and with a trace of French accent. "Ellen! Ellen!"

She drew back her head and offered me her mouth. I fumblingly covered it with mine. My tongue darted inside, and she sucked on it feverishly. At the same time, her breasts and pelvis pressed even harder against me.

I don't know what the real Jean-Claude would have done at this point. But the Damon version of Jean-Claude suddenly became an unleashed bull-in-heat. I pulled her down onto the couch with me, still kissing her, and cupped one of those fantastic breasts in my hand. Simultaneously, my knees maneuvered into place between her legs, wedging them open, and my free hand began stroking the firm, sexy flesh of her thigh.

"Ellen!" I groaned, trying to keep the French accent, but suspecting that I was failing. "Let's not waste another moment! Let's make love!"

If it bothered her that I was slipping out of character, she didn't show it. Still sucking feverishly at my tongue, she spread her thighs wider. At the same time, her fingers went to work on my fly.

My hand found its way to her womanhood. I caressed her through her panties for a moment, then eased my fingers through one of the panty-legs and invaded her quivering cleft. She writhed ecstatically beneath me, all the while continuing to murmur, "Jean-Claude! Jean-Claude! Jean-Claude!"

I eased the waistband of her panties over her hips. She shifted her weight to make things easier for me, and I very rapidly slid the panties midway down her thighs. By this time, she had also managed to release my manhood from the prison of my jockey shorts. She clutched its nakedness with a desperateness that made me thirst for her all the more.

I couldn't get her panties all the way off without moving out from between her legs, so I shifted my position and lay alongside her on the couch. She raised her knees and brought her legs together. I quickly disposed of the panties, and used my free hand to tug my trousers open.

The panties now off, she spread her thighs again. The hem of her mini was hiked way up over her hips, and the splendor of her blonde Mound of Venus beckoned me. I answered the call. My fingers clutched at her superb buttocks as my tongue discovered the sweetness of her love-channel.

Her legs were over my shoulders; her thighs were squeezing lovingly against the sides of my face. Her hips rocked back and forth in response to the thrusts of my tongue. Her whole body seemed to be shaking with excitement.

"Jean-Claude!" she sighed. "Oh, Jean-Claude!" Then, after a moment: "Darling, take me! Oh, please take me!"

I didn't need a second invitation. Quicker than a flash, I bobbed up from my prone position and threw myself on top

33

of her. As part of the same movement, I shimmied my trousers and shorts down to my knees, maneuvered my knees into place between her thighs, and covered her mouth with mine.

"Cut!" cried a voice somewhere outside the range of my immediate interests.

I ignored it and manipulated my sword into position for the stab that really grabs.

"Cut!" cried the voice again.

I still refused to pay attention to it, but suddenly my sword was without a scabbard. Beautiful, love-hungry, devoted Ellen had become Robbi Randall again, and she was struggling to get out from under me.

"Cut, Damon!" repeated the voice as a pair of surprisingly strong hands tugged at my shoulders. "Cut! The scene is over! Cut!"

With Walrus-moustache's help, Robbi managed to slither off the couch. Seizing up her panties, she retreated to a post in front of his desk. I fought him a moment, then realizing that it was futile to fight, flopped over on my back. "If I ever find a voodoo doll that looks like you," I told him, "I'm going to stick every pin I can find into it."

Ignoring the comment, he told Robbi that she could leave the room. Then he ambled back to his seat and refilled his glass with Johnnie Walker Black.

Dejectedly, I pulled my pants back on. "You're a real buddy, you walrus-moustached son of a bitch," I grunted. "You're a buddy and a half."

He smiled brightly. "Cheer up, Damon. You can always do Take Two after your mission is completed. Meanwhile, be thankful for small favors. If I wanted to, I could've called 'Cut' a lot sooner than I did."

I buckled my belt and slouched down in my seat. "You also could've let us go the full route. She certainly was ready."

His smile broadened. "And she'll be ready again once the mission is over. Now, speaking of the mission, let's speak some more about the mission, okay?"

It's a wise general who knows when to retreat. "Go ahead," I growled. "Speak away."

He sipped his drink. "All right, if you insist. As I was saying before we got sidetracked, Robbi Randall persuaded Lady Brice-Bennington to accept her as a repentant sinner, and promptly was welcomed with open arms into the Friends of

Decency. For the next several months, she worked actively on behalf of the Friends—typing letters of protest to newspaper editors about erotic books which were circulating in London, recording antisexual speeches to be broadcast by radio stations sympathetic to the Friends' cause, et cetera, et cetera, et cetera. At the same time, she kept her eyes and ears open, and reported to The Coxe Foundation regularly on the comings and goings of Lady Brice-Bennington and her fellow-travelers. We have three entire filing cabinets chock-full of her reports."

"What do they reveal?"

"Unfortunately nothing that we didn't know already. We now have millions of words describing the activities of the Friends of Decency, but not one word which in any way connects The Big Prig or any of her Friends with Andi Gleason, Diane Dionne or the Communists's British spy network. That, dear Damon, is why we called upon you. We feel that Robbi Randall, because of the nature of her cover-role as an enthusiastic member of the Friends, is not really in a position to explore the channels which you, in the cover-role of a Doubting Thomas, might explore. So we're going to send you to London to conduct a survey in cooperation with the Friends of Decency, and we're hoping that you'll be able to come up with some of the answers that Robbi Randall couldn't come up with—all the while managing concurrently to spirit Andi Gleason and Diane Dionne out of the country, and finding out precisely what if anything the Commies know about the B-bomb."

I frowned. "What makes you think that the Friends will want to cooperate with me in this proposed survey?"

He smiled. "I said before that if there's anything a repentant sinner thrives on it's the recognition of another repentant sinner. I might have added that there's one thing most repentant sinners thrive on even more—namely, the prospects of winning a convert. And, of course, the more notorious a sinner the prospective convert is, the better the repentant sinner likes it."

"I'm afraid I don't quite see what you're driving at."

"Just this: Robbi Randall, after she had gained full acceptance as a loyal Friend of Decency, sold Lady Brice-Bennington on the idea that what the Friends really needed was some scientific evidence that the free dissemination of erotic literature is a principal cause of sexual permissiveness in contemporary London. Robbi then volunteered to recruit

35

you, the world's foremost sexologist—and, of course, one of the world's most outspoken sexual liberals—to supply that evidence."

"But," I protested, "there *is* no proof that erotic literature is connected with sex crimes—and there's a great deal of proof that it isn't."

He smiled. "You know that, and I know that, but The Big Prig doesn't know it. Like all zealous missionaries, she's completely convinced of the rightness of her cause. She sincerely believes that there is a connection, as she's been preaching all these years, and she's certain that any genuinely valid scientific study will prove it. Consequently, when Robbi suggested that the Friends of Decency hire you to conduct a study—under their auspices and under their supervision, of course—Lady Brice-Bennington thought the idea was simply ginger-peachy."

"And that's why Robbi came back to America? To recruit me?"

"Not quite. Although you were unaware of it, she recruited you by mail. Her letters addressed to you actually were sent to The Coxe Foundation, and she received replies bearing your signature—forged by experts, of course."

"That's what I like about you guys. You're so ethical."

He ignored the comment. "In your replies, you accepted the Friends' invitation to study the relationship between erotic literature and sexual permissiveness in contemporary London. Once a fee had been agreed upon—a fee of a thousand dollars per month plus expenses, in case you're interested—you said that you were all ready to go. Robbi then was dispatched by Lady Brice-Bennington to meet you here in the States and bring you to London, which she will do very soon."

Something about the way he said "very soon" struck me as curious. "How soon?" I asked.

He glanced at his watch. "Well, you should arrive there by nine tomorrow morning. My mobile field office should deposit you at the airport within the hour, and your flight is scheduled to leave at ten p.m., our time."

I gulped. "But I'm expected back at the office party. And I haven't got anything with me but the clothes I'm wearing."

"You can buy all the clothes you need in London. They've got excellent tailors there, and in case you forgot, you're on an unlimited expense account. As for the office party, we've sent someone to replace you. Since everything there is being carried on in the dark, I don't think anyone will miss you.

And when it comes time for you to take your date home, our man will simply tell her that you didn't feel well and asked him to pinch-hit for you." He looked at me with a mischievous twinkling in his eyes. "I guess I've answered all your objections, haven't I?"

I didn't answer.

I couldn't.

What's there to say when your captors have you by the proverbials and both of you know it?

CHAPTER THREE

Pan-Am's big Boeing 707 lifted off right on schedule, and yours truly, Dr. Rod Damon, reluctant superspy for the United States of America, was on his way to Merrie Olde England.

But Superspy Damon was in a mood anything but merrie.

For one thing, I've never been particularly nuts about flying. I'd long before passed the stage where flying frightened me. But I'd never been able to develop a frame of mind whereunder I considered it fun—as all the airline ads said it was—to pass six hours sitting cramped-up in a too-narrow seat with too little legroom and nowhere to go for relaxation except the bathroom.

For another, I was far from ecstatic about being tapped for another mission on behalf of The Coxe Foundation. Back at the laboratory of the League for Sexual Dynamics, my colleagues were putting into practice all the new twists and turns of sex which they had discovered during their previous three hundred and sixty-four days of dedicated research. And I, their leader, had walked out on them to play another round of spy games with The Big Prig and the Communists. Among the fates I would have accepted with only slightly more displeasure were leukemia, cirrhosis of the liver and cancer of the pancreas.

My mood, of course, would have been brighter if my traveling companion had been a bit friendlier. But, despite her abundance of passion when she was playing Ellen to my Jean-Claude, Robbi Randall had gone ice-cold again once Walrus-moustache's little scene had ended, and, try though I might, I had been unable to defrost her.

Let the record note: I *did* try. For more than half an hour before takeoff and a good hour afterwards, I used all the rehetoric at my command to convince her that she would have plenty of time to get back into her role as a Damon-hating Friend of Decency once the plane began circling Heathrow Airport for its London landing. But I might as well have tried to sell her the Brooklyn Bridge. She did talk freely and in great detail about the comings and goings of Lady Brice-Bennington and the Friends. But her manner was strictly business, and the contempt-filled tone of her voice served as a constant reminder that she regarded me—at least while she was playing the Friend role—as a creature just slightly less loathsome than Hitler or Atilla the Hun.

Finally, somewhere between Iceland and Newfoundland, I abandoned my attempts at getting through to her and buried myself in the dossiers which Walrus-moustache had given me to study before I began my actual work on the case. They covered essentially the same terrain he had covered in his briefing, but in considerably greater detail. I read them twice, start to finish, then reread several sections that struck me as sort of curious.

Especially curious, I thought, was the history of The Big Prig herself. She had acquired a ladyship via marriage to Lord Brice-Bennington, but previously had been of working-class background. She had come to London from her native Dorchester ten years ago, at age eighteen, and had gone the secretary-receptionist-filing clerk route for a year or two before moving in with the so-called smart set. Then she had gone the playgirl route, presumably subsisting on gifts from her lovers, for another two or three years.

Somewhere or other along the line, she evidently had decided that the sweet life wasn't as sweet as it seemed. In any case, five years ago, she stopped being a playgirl and formed the Friends of Decency. She got her initial financing from religious organizations and other groups traditionally opposed to sexual permissiveness, then built the Friends into a financial powerhouse which, through private contributions, now enjoyed an income of better than a million dollars a year. She herself, along with other staff members, took only a modest salary; the rest of the money was channeled into the Friends' lawsuits and propaganda activities.

A year after forming the Friends, she married Lord Brice-Bennington, who, I guessed, had met her in the course of her work and had decided that she was that ultra-desirable sort of old-fashioned "nice" girl that seemed to be in ever-dwindling supply nowadays. Lord B-B at the time had been a thirty-five-year-old bachelor who kept pretty much out of the social mainstream, preferring to devote his time to fox hunting, card games at exlusive gentlemen's clubs, and similar old-school aristocratic pursuits. He never took a visibly active part in any of the Friends' activities; but he evidently was both pleased with and proud of his wife's efforts to stamp out sex and sin in the British Empire.

What struck me as particularly curious about all this was Lady B-B's sudden—or, as may have been the case, grad-ual—conversion from the ways of sin to the ways of righteousness. I could understand that a playgirl might grow disenchanted with her life and decide to turn over a new leaf. But I couldn't quite see how a playgirl like Lady B-B, who ap-peared to be a typical working-class girl, unencumbered by the moral strictures and social goals of the middle class, would be motivated to shift gears so dramatically in midstream. If she had been the daughter of a clergyman, for example, or if she had been raised in an extremely puritan-nical atmosphere, her about-face might have made sense. But according to Walrus-moustache's dossier, her parents were far from religious, and she herself had not been a regular churchgoer before forming the Friends.

Also—and, of course, I am biased on this count—I couldn't imagine how anyone who had really gotten into sex, anyone who had really gained an appreciation of what a won-derful thing it is, could ever go sour on it, no matter what her past influences. The examples of Mary Magdalen, St. Paul, Emperor Constantine, et. al., notwithstanding, I found it im-possible to conceive of anyone who had really enjoyed sex ever becoming a bluenose.

Another thing that struck me as curious was the tie-in be-tween Lady B-B's campaign against Smythe and Whelan and the Communists' interest in getting Smythe and Whelan turned out of office. According to Walrus-moustache's dossier, Lord B-B was a diehard conservative, a man whose view were so far to the right that he made America's

Goldwater look, in comparison, like a flaming liberal. Even if Lord B-B shared his wife's opinions on the evils of sex and the alleged connection between free disemmination of erotic literature and sexual permissiveness, would he want her to fight so diligently against two staunch anti-Communists like Smythe and Whelan just because they were pro-sex? I didn't think so.

Was Lady B-B's campaign against Smythe and Whelan being undertaken contrary to her husband's wishes? I couldn't imagine that either. A fundamental rule—indeed, a standing operating procedure—in old-school marriages of the sort which Lord and Lady B-B seemed to have is that the husband calls all the shots. So where did Lady B-B, The Big Prig, come off playing right into the hands of the Commies—who, on the face of things, seemed to be her husband's *bêtes noirs.*

Finally among the things that struck me curious was the business of Andi Gleason and Diane Dionne being used to set Smythe and Whelan up for a scandal. I couldn't really imagine the Friends, who presumably would adhere to the old Christian dictum that the end never justifies the means, arranging a sexual frame-up. And yet, long before the Coxe Foundation had reason to suspect Communist involvement, one highly placed member of the Friends had over the space of two weeks made three visits to the Soho strip-joint where Andi Gleason had worked before becoming a full-time prostitute, while another highly placed Friend had during the same period attended several pot parties at which Diane Dionne was present. If these Friends hadn't been trying to arrange a frame-up, what were they doing on the scene? And if, contrary to my expectations, they *had* been trying to arrange a frame-up, where did the Communists fit into the picture?

Walrus-moustache seemed to think that it was the Commies who arranged the frame-up. This theory, on the face of things, seemed more plausible. But, if the frame-up had been the Commies' doing, where did the two highly placed Friends who were rubbing elbows with Andi and Diane fit in? If the Commies were framing Smythe and Whelan in the interest of getting information on the B-Bomb, they certainly wouldn't want the Friends to be hip to the Smythe-Whelan-Andi-Diane liaison, because the Friends almost certainly would set off a scandal before the Commies could find out what they wanted to know.

Had the Friends possibly learned of the liaison through their own sources, and had their two emissaries been frequenting the netherworld simply to gain more information? Quite possible. But, if they now had enough on Smythe and Whelan to set off scandal—and it was safe to assume that they did, since The Coxe Foundation had acquired *its* evidence of hanky-panky in a lot shorter time than the Friends had had to acquire theirs—why hadn't they set off the scandal already? As Walrus-moustache had pointed out, the sooner a scandalmonger triggers a scandal like this, the better off he is.

I checked this question out with Robbi Randall, who patronizingly granted me an audience of three minutes in which to answer it. Putting down the copy of *The Life of Saint Maria Goretti* in which she appeared to have been totally absorbed, she advised me that, active though she was in the Friends, she was not yet close enough to Lady B-B to have been apprised of any developments in the scandal department, if in fact there were such developments on the Friends' side of the fence.

This left me right back where I had started—nowhere. And since I obviously couldn't get anywhere without doing some in-person fishing around, I decided to stop speculating for the time being. Tucking Walrus-moustache's dossiers back into my briefcase, I put the briefcase under my seat, maneuvered myself into as comfortable a position as I could manage in my cramped quarters, closed my eyes, and tried to fall asleep.

But sleep wouldn't come. One reason why it wouldn't was because the couple in the row of seats behind me had suddenly become involved in a very animated discussion about the alleged superiority of the London theater over the Broadway theater; I couldn't have been less interested in their conversation, but they were talking so loud that, try though I might, I couldn't shut their voices out of my consciousness. Another reason was that Robbi's reading light was shining in my eyes. And a third reason was Robbi's magnificent breasts. While she had abandoned the see-through she had been wearing earlier in favor of a conservative tweed jacket which concealed her charms much more effectively, the twin bulges in the jacket—which were right in my line of vision—served as a constant reminder of what I had viewed in full, unadorned splendor such a while before. By closing my eyes I could remove the immediate stimulus; but I couldn't erase my memory of those marvelous thirty-eights—so, the absence of stimulus notwithstanding, the response was still there.

I finally gave up on my attempts to sleep and decided to

41

make another stab at defrosting Robbi. "Uh, sweetheart," I said fumblingly, "can I talk to you about something?"

Marking her place in *The Life of Saint Maria Goretti* with her finger, she gave me the sort of look mothers give little boys who have to go to the bathroom in public places where there don't seem to be any bathrooms around. "To you, Damon, I am not 'sweetheart,' I am 'Miss Randall,'" she replied tartly. "Now what's bothering you this time?"

"Well," I stumbled, "I've, ah, been sort of thinking, ah, that the time is going to come on this mission, ah, when we're going to have to work, ah, pretty closely together . . ."

"Stop pronouncing the spaces between your words and get to the point."

"Well, ah—excuse me—when I do get to the bottom of this business about who put Andi Gleason and Diane Dionne up to framing Smythe and Whelan, you and I, ah—excuse me—may have to make a fast getaway, ah, together."

"So?"

"Well, if that time comes and you're still very deep in the down-with-Damon bag, will you be able to change character and become my ally on such short notice?"

"Certainly."

"How will you be able to do it—without some practice?"

"Let *me* worry about the now. Now flake off, will you? I'm reading."

I let a little of my anger and impatience show through. "No, I won't flake off. If you've got to be a fourteen-karat bitch with me twenty-four hours a day just to stay in character for The Big Prig's benefit, I don't think you'll be able to make the transition when the chips are down."

The corners of her mouth curved upward in a small, superior little smile. "You saw how fast I could make a transition back in the van, didn't you?"

"Yeah, but you had Walrus-moustache directing you then. You won't have him in London when the you-know-what hits the fan."

"I'll manage on my own."

"I can't take your word for it. I want proof."

"What sort of proof?"

"Make the transition now. Pretend that we're together in London, and that we've got to escape together to a plane that's waiting to take us back to the States. I've just confiscated the negatives that prove Smythe and Whelan have been carrying on with Andi Gleason and Diane Dionne"—

as I spoke my voice took on something of the directorial tone which Walrus-moustache had used earlier—"and the Communist plot has been foiled. But the Communists have learned that you and I are working for The Coxe Foundation. As we sit hunched together in a dark corner of Lady Brice-Bennington's mansion, our enemies are stalking through the corridors, guns in hand, looking for us and——"

She frowned. "Damon, if you aren't a better lover than a film director, heaven help the League for Sexual Dynamics."

"I'm new at being a director. Give me a chance."

"Forget it. If you really *have* to have your stupid little demonstration, and if the only way I can get you to leave me alone is to give it to you, I will. But don't make my job harder. I'll direct myself. You just sit there and wait for the results."

Appropriately chastised, I sat and waited. Dog-earing her page in *The Life of Saint Maria Goretti*, Robbi slid the book under her seat. Then, covering her face with her hands, she leaned forward like a guru going into a trance.

I watched, fascinated. Very slowly, but nonetheless very visibly, her body seemed to go through a series of changes. The stiffness with which she had been sitting while in her Friend-of-Decency role gradually gave way to a seemingly total relaxation. Then a nervous tension seemed to take possession of her, and she cowered in the seat, as if both of us actually were hunched together in that dark corner of Lady B-B's mansion that I had been talking about, while gun-wielding Commies stalked the corridors outside.

Her hands now came away from her face, and her eyes found mine. They looked at me with unnervingly genuine fear, and yet with what appeared to be complete trust. She brought one hand to my forearm.

"Rod," she whispered tensely, "do you think we'll really make it?"

I found myself, to my astonishment, getting right into character with her. "We'll make it, baby," I Humphrey Bogart-ed. "Don't worry."

She brought her face closer to mine. "I believe you. I don't know why, but I believe you."

I suddenly was aware of the sweet, subtle scent of her perfume. She excited me, not with the excitement of mere sex, but with the excitement of a much deeper emotional bond. "Robbi," I said softly, "I love you." And, incredible as it may seem, I sincerely felt at the moment that I did.

43

She leaned closer toward me, and her lips touched my cheek. "I love you, Rod," she purred. "And I want you. I want you desperately. I want to make love to you."

My fingers found one of the buttons on her tweed jacket. I deftly unbuttoned it, and my hand slipped inside, closing around the soft, firm flesh of her exquisite breast. The nipple tensed under my touch, and her face pressed more firmly against mine. "We will make love," I said. "Just as soon as we get away from here. And we *will* get away, Robbi. I know we will."

"I know we will too, Rod. I know we will too."

For a moment we silently shared the delicious tenderness of our union. Then her lips neared mine, and she whispered, "Kiss me, Rod. Gently. Kiss me."

I kissed her. Her lips parted slightly, and my tongue slipped between them. I gripped her bare breast more firmly, and, astonishing though it was, I found myself thinking that I never in my life had loved a girl more.

We held the kiss for maybe thirty seconds. Then she slowly backed away.

"Robbi," I murmured, "you're beautiful."

She looked at me and smiled. The fear had gone from her eyes now. But, unexplainably, the affection and devotion that had been there suddenly seemed to be going also. Her smile, at first one of incredible warmth and tenderness, rapidly was becoming a grin of triumph. She gingerly extracted my hand from inside her blouse and pushed it toward me as though it were a bag of garbage.

"Well, Damon," she said, rebuttoning the jacket, "you got your demonstration. Now cool it, okay?"

I was crushed—really crushed. Only my pride kept me from begging her to play the game a little longer.

"Robbi," I said softly, "you've proved beyond a doubt that you're a great actress." Forcing a self-confident expression of superiority, I added bitterly, "But you've also proved that you're a bitch *par excellence*. For your sake, I hope there's a real person somewhere beneath all that talent. For my own sake, I don't think I'm ever going to take the trouble of trying to find out."

She took *The Life of Saint Maria Goretti* back out from under the seat. "Your loss, Damon," she snapped. "Now flake off."

I did the only sensible thing under the circumstances. Trying hard not to show my real feelings, I flaked off.

44

The prettiest of the plane's six stewardesses was at the moment taking an illegal cigarette break back in the galley. I ambled over to her, turned on the old Damon charm, chatted about the sort of banal topics which stews the world over seem to find so fascinating—like how she enjoyed flying and which of the world's cities she liked most—and entered her New York phone number in my little black book. Then, after polishing off a trio of double Johnnie Walker Blacks, I returned to my seat, ignored Robbi Randall completely, maneuvered my body into a semi-foetal ball and, thanks mainly to the Johnnie Walker Blacks, conked out like a light.

I woke to find a not-too-gentle hand shaking my shoulder. Rubbing the sleep from my eyes, I discovered that the hand belonged to Robbi.

"I hope I'm not interrupting a wet dream," she said curtly, "but we happen to have landed in London."

I straightened my clothes, picked up my briefcase and followed her out of the plane. Waiting for us at the baggage rack were two women. One was a schoolmarmish type in her fifties. The other was a considerably younger woman whom I recognized immediately as none other than The Big Prig herself.

I'd had so many surprises over the past twelve hours that I couldn't really say that I was flabbergasted at Lady B-B's appearance. But I was, to put it mildly, taken aback.

There had been two snapshots of her in Walrus-moustache's dossier. The first, taken during her playgirl days, was a head-and-shoulders shot of a pretty and sexy—though overly made-up—young swinger who certainly would be worth a roll in the hay but hardly would inspire more than passing interest. The second, taken much more recently, showed a frumpy-looking girl in her late twenties whose face, unimproved by make-up, was totally bland, and whose bodily assets, if indeed there were any, were concealed by a baggy black dress the hem of which fell just above her ankles.

Now, in person, The Big Prig stood as living proof that photographs can be deceiving. Her face, untouched by the cosmeticist's hand, wasn't exactly the sort that launches a thousand ships. But there was something very natural and attractive about it. The sexiness that had shown through in the first snapshot was still there, but in a much more subtle and exciting way. The prettiness, though camouflaged by a huge pair of round, rimless spectacles, was also apparent.

She wore an ankle-length black dress very similar to the

one she had worn in the second snapshot, and she was obviously heavily corseted beneath it. The fullness of the dress and the heaviness of the corseting made it impossible for me to appraise her body accurately. But her overall form was good, and my practiced eye perceived bulges here and crevasses which suggested that, while they might not be perfectly placed, the raw materials of a groovy bod were nonetheless very present.

Robbi Randall performed the introductions. The fiftyish schoolmarm-type, whose name turned out to be Gretchen Stark, was presented as executive director of the Friends and secretary of the London Council of Religious Organizations Opposed to the Disemmination of Filth. She took my hand as though she were afraid it would contaminate her, gave it a perfunctory squeeze, then dropped it like a hot potato.

The Big Prig was considerably more cordial. While she didn't exactly fall panting into my arms, she did squeeze my hand firmly, and the look in her pretty blue eyes suggested that she was not unfriendly toward me and perhaps even a little fascinated by me. "Doctor Damon," she smiled affably, "welcome to the enemy camp."

"Enemy, Lady Brice-Bennington?" I replied, letting my charm ooze through. "I think not. A beautiful woman like yourself can never be my enemy. She may accept my friendship or reject it, but, in either case, I shall always think of her as my friend."

Robbi Randall's smirk let me know what *she* thought of my Captain Gallant approach. Frumpy Gretchen Stark was equally—and visibly—unimpressed. But I wasn't pitching Robbi and Gretchen at the moment; I was pitching The Big Prig—and, from what I could see, she liked my pitch.

"You're a very charming man, Doctor," she said. "Small wonder you've managed to entice so many tender young innocents into your boudoir."

I smiled. "Many there have been, your ladyship, and most were tender, but few were young and fewer still innocent."

Robbi almost choked on that one. Gretchen Stark turned away as though she were going to vomit. But The Big Prig responded with a chuckle that told me I was really on her wave length.

"Tell me, Doctor," she said, "how do you feel about the work you're going to do for us?"

My eyebrows arched quizzically. "How do I feel, madame? I don't quite understand the question. Work is work. One

46

generally doesn't have feelings about it one way or the other."

"I should think you would. After all, your studies in the past have been decidedly pro-sexual. Now you've been commissioned to conduct a study which will prove that the free dissemination of erotic literature is a principal cause of sexual permissiveness in contemporary London. This conclusion flies in the face of everything you've written so far."

"Not so fast, madame. As I understand the commission, I'm going to conduct a study which will *attempt* to determine if there actually *is* a connection between the free dissemination of erotic literature and sexual permissiveness. A scientist never concludes anything until all the evidence has been assembled."

"You're being semantic, Damon." Her tone grew a shade cooler. "We both know that there is a connection."

I smiled superiorly. "Science, madame, knows only what has been proven. So far nothing has been proven on this subject. That's why I consented to conduct the study."

Gretchen Stark decided to put her two pence worth in. "I don't know anything about science, Doctor, but I know what I see. In nineteen sixty-seven, more than sixty percent of the young people arrested in Great Britain for sex crimes were found to have erotic materials either on their person or in their domiciles. The statistics of your Federal Bureau of Investigation in the United States are quite similar. How do you explain that?"

"Miss Stark," I replied evenly, "I would venture to say that nearly one hundred percent of all murderers arrested in the United States and Great Britain during nineteen sixty-seven were found to have toothbrushes either on their person or in their domiciles. Does this prove a connection between the free dissemination of dental hygiene devices and homicide?"

"That's not a valid comparison, Damon, and you know it," said Robbi Randall.

"It is a valid comparison," I replied. "Correlation does not prove causation. The causatory relationship of one variable to another must be established independently of the mere harmonious existence of both variables." I closed the sentence with a smile that said: How do you like *them* apples?

My little excursion into jargonese accomplished the desired effect. Since neither Lady B-B, Gretchen Stark nor Robbi Randall knew what the hell I was talking about, they couldn't pursue their arguments any further.

To Lady B-B I said, "Under the terms of our agreement,

47

madame, I am going to assemble data which may or may not prove that there is a relationship between erotica and sexual permissiveness. My data will be scientifically valid, and you'll have the right to turn them over to other scientists of your own choosing to corroborate or deny their validity. The conclusions I draw will be equally valid, whatever they may be, and you'll also have the opportunity of having independent scientists evaluate them. Once I've given them to you, you can use them as you wish. If they support your cause, you can publicize them. If they don't, you can shove them"—I curbed the impulse to finish the sentence with the phrase that really was on my mind—"into a filing cabinet somewhere."

The Big Prig smiled, "That's fair enough, Damon. But let me remind you that we'll be supervising you very closely. Your sexual views are well known to us, and we're not unaware that you might be tempted to twist the statistics to favor your own point of view,"

"Supervise me as closely as you like, madame," I purred. My eyes fixing to hers meaningfully, I added, "I'd like nothing more than to be supervised very closely by you."

At this point, as if on cue, Robbi Randall's luggage arrived on the baggage rack. A redcap took it in tow, and our party adjourned to Lady Brice-Bennington's sedan in the airport parking lot. Robbi Randall drove, and Gretchen Stark shared the front seat with her. I shared the back set with The Big Prig.

Helping her through the door, I gripped her at the bicep, carefully letting the back of my hand brush against her breast. She jerked away from my touch, but not before there had been a good five or six seconds of uninterrupted contact. I couldn't be sure whether she liked being touched by me or whether she just had slow reflexes, but judging from everything I had seen so far, I was betting on the former. One thing was certain: unless I had completely lost my ability to judge a woman's sexual response, Lady Brice-Bennington was anything but The Big Prig she was made out to be.

Once inside the car, I sat square against her. My briefcase gave me the excuse to do so. It took up the space between me and the edge of the seat. As had been the case when I touched her breast, she lingered for a few seconds before moving away from me. I resolved that I'd make it a point to get off somewhere with her alone—where Gretchen Stark and Robbi Randall wouldn't be witnesses to what happened between us—at the earliest possible moment. I suspected that when I

48

did I'd learn a lot more about The Big Prig than her Friends of Decency had ever dreamed there was to learn.

The trip from the airport to the mansion which served as both Lady B-B's home and the headquarters for her Friends took an hour and a half. We passed the time discussing administrative details about my proposed study. I hadn't had time to work out a detailed prospectus, but I was an old enough hand at the sex survey game that I was able to ad-lib convincingly.

I said that I wanted to conduct in-depth interviews with three random samples of contemporary London young men and women. One sample would be made up of persons who, in response to a mail survey, reported that they had not engaged in sexual intercourse before marriage. Another sample would be made up of persons who reported that they had engaged in sexual intercourse before marriage. The third sample would be drawn from London's demimonde of prostitutes, pimps, strippers and others of professed libertine proclivities. All respondents would be questioned about the nature and extent of their erotic reading. Then, when the statistics had been assembled, an attempt would be made to establish parallels between reading habits and sexual behavior.

Lady B-B accepted the plan with one qualification: she wanted me to balance the demimonde sample with a sample of students at church-operated schools. From a scientific point of view, her request was unreasonable because the ages and domicile status of the school sample wouldn't be parallel to the ages and domicile status of the other samples. But in the interest of harmony I accepted the qualification.

We then worked out such details as how the random samples would be drawn, who would do the actual selecting of respondents, who would perform the clerical work, et cetera. By this time, we were at the mansion, and, over lunch, we concluded our administrative arrangements. Lady B-B then gave me a guided tour of the mansion and the Friends' headquarters after which she volunteered to escort me to my hotel. Out of a sense of mischief, I selected the Hotel Eros on Shaftesbury Avenue, a piquant touch which seemed to amuse rather than annoy her.

It was now four p.m. and I was dog-tired, but I didn't want to say goodbye to The Big Prig before I had had a chance to ask a few important questions. She accepted my invitation for tea, and as we sat across from each other at a small table in the hotel breakfast room, I went to work.

49

"Have you always believed," I asked, "that sex is such a horrible thing?"

Her eyes took on a wistful look. "Once, Damon, when I was much younger, I expected it to be supremely beautiful. But, of course, I had been misled by the propaganda of eroticists such as yourself. I since have come to realize that it is vastly overrated."

"Did you give it a fair try?"

Her smile was that of one who has gone the full route and now speaks with unimpeachable authority. "Yes, sad to say, I did. For several years I lent myself shamelessly to every debauchery. It was only after wallowing in the very depths of filth and depravity that I saw the light, and it perhaps is because I sunk as low as I did that I now am as devoted as I am to the cause of purity and decency."

"Tell me something about your experiences and about how you came to hold your present views."

Without embarrassment—in fact, almost with pride—she described her peccadilloes as a playgirl. Her tone was that of a penitent who while condemning his sins also rejoices in them because their magnitude makes repentance and atonement all the more meaningful. I listened carefully to the recitation, and prodded her as she went along with questions designed to illuminate other areas of her life. After an hour of tactful questioning, I had elicited an autobiography which paralleled very closely the background information in Walrus-moustache's dossier.

I was strongly tempted to ask if during her many sexual meanderings she had ever experienced orgasm. I rather suspected that she hadn't. But I was afraid that I'd lose rapport with her if I questioned her that intimately at this early stage of the game, so I held back.

I also wanted to ask about her interest in getting Smythe and Whelan turned out of office, and whether her husband opposed her support of the pro-Communist candidates. But I didn't want to tip my hand on this count just yet, so I let the question remain unasked.

I did permit myself one little shot in the dark. "Lady Brice-Bennington," I said, "this morning when I first saw you at the airport, I experienced a feeling of warmth toward you, a very tender feeling, one not entirely sexual but at least partly sexual. With all due respect, I must say that I also got the impression that you responded to this feeling, and that you felt a certain warmth toward me. Am I wrong?"

She blushed a deep crimson.

I smiled. "I'm not wrong, am I?"

It took her a long moment to answer. "Doctor Damon," she said finally, "I won't deny that I'm somewhat attracted to you. But, of course, the sexual impulse is strong even in those of us who realize what a dangerous thing sex really is. The difference between humans and animals is that humans control their sexual impulses."

I decided to quit while I was ahead. Shifting the conversation to less intimate areas, I chatted with her for another fifteen minutes. Then, promising to see her at the mansion the following day to begin my study, I bade her goodbye.

The time was now five fifteen. I was tired enough that I could have slept right through until the next afternoon. But I knew that I had work to do and that it had to be done fast if the Commies were to be prevented from getting their hands on the B-bomb. I permitted myself a six-hour nap. Then, after wolfing down a plate of cold roast beef in a pub off Piccadilly Circus, I hightailed it to the Soho strip-joint where Andi Gleason had done her thing before she went the full-time prostie route. The odds against finding her there, I knew, were far from good. But, good odds or not, I had to start somewhere. There was no better place than The Safari Club, and no better time than the present.

CHAPTER FOUR

When you're in the spy business, your worst enemy is the Law of Averages. Your main activity is tracking down leads —looking for people, for scraps of information, or occasionally for theories that will help you get to the bottom of the mystery you're trying to solve. But you can only be in one place at one time, and the Law of Averages says that more often than not you're going to be in the wrong place.

But the Law is like a woman—fickle. It doesn't give you a fifty-one percent run of bad luck and then a forty-nine percent run of good. It may stack the cards against you one hundred percent of the time in case after case after case, and then, on your next case, hand you what you're looking for right on the proverbial silver platter.

Evidently the time had now come in my spy career for the Law to throw me a bone. At The Safari Club, Andi Gleason was handed to me on a silver platter. Clarification: She wasn't literally handed to me, but she was literally on a silver platter.

The Safari Club, as I learned after I paid a ten-pound "temporary membership" fee and another thirty shillings as a cover charge, was one of those London specialty clubs that offer bizarre sex in exotic settings to anyone who can pay the price. Walrus-moustache had called it a strip-joint, and strictly speaking, that's what it was. But it bore no resemblance whatsoever to the sleazy gin mills which most Americans think of when they hear the term, "strip-joint." True, girls took off their clothes there. But they did a lot more than just disrobe. And the atmosphere in which they performed was anything but sleazy.

The place was roughly half the size of a basketball court. The center of one side was given over to a stage about twelve feet square. Runways on both sides led to a pair of doors covered with strings of beads. The rest of the area was dotted with small wooden tables and chairs.

The decor, as befit the name of the place, was African. The walls were covered with vines and live tropical plants, and the floor was carpeted with a wall-to-wall rug which, to my unpracticed eye appeared to be genuine leopardskin. The tables and chairs were exquisitely hand-crafted, with carvings of the heads of jungle beasts on all the arms and legs. For an ashtray, each table had a carved-out human skull, which the maître d' assured me was the real thing. And the rum punch I ordered was served in a mug which I was assured was genuine ivory.

I arrived just in time for the first show of the night. No sooner had my drink been served than a quartet of barebreasted Negresses came scurrying down the runways, beating out tribal polyrhythms on native wooden percussion instruments. Once they were in place on stage, two muscular Negro men carrying conga drums made their way down the runways. Then the men squatted at the foot of the stage and beat out a furious conga rhythm while the girls did a frantic dance.

The whole bit was authentic enough, I suppose, but it didn't strike me as particularly erotic. I glanced periodically at the stage to make sure I wasn't missing out on any dramatic new developments, but I spent most of my time looking around the room at the other customers. Among the items in Walrus-moustache's dossier on Andi Gleason had been several photos of her, and a dozen other photos of Soho pimps and prosties who were known to be her associates. I was hoping I'd spot one or more of them, whom I then could ask to introduce me to her.

No one in the rapidly filling club resembled anyone in the photos. There were a few couples in the thirty-to-fifty age range—all extremely well-dressed, and, judging from their rapt interest in what was happening onstage, newcomers to the circuit. But the rest of the audience consisted mainly of fiftyish, sixtyish and even seventyish men—all stag. Some came in pairs, but the majority came solo and were paired off at tables for two or four by the maître d'. They seemed about as uninterested in the tribal dance as I was, presumably because they were regular patrons who knew that the real fireworks weren't quite ready to start.

The girls on stage finished their dance and the two conga players stopped playing. An offstage microphoned voice announced that we had just witnessed an ancient Nigerian rain dance and that we now could see a Bantusi premarital preparation dance.

The conga players resumed playing. Three of the girls formed a circle in the center of the stage and squatted down Indian-style, whacking away at their wooden percussion instruments. The fourth girl stood in the middle of the circle and went into slow, langurous series of motions that resembled the Hawaiian hula except that her movements were more vertical than horizontal.

At this point the maître d' ushered a monocled gent of about sixty-five to my table. The gent gave me a polite nod, then turned his attention to the stage. His expression was one of mild interest, sort of like the expression of a horseplayer watching the next race's entries being paraded toward the starting gate.

I took another look around the room. Most of the tables were filled by this time. I could clearly see the faces of seventy-five percent of the audience. If Andi Gleason and/or any of the others I was looking for were present, they weren't among my seventy-five percent.

Gradually the intensity of the conga rhythms began to build. I returned my attention to the stage. The star performer in the Bantusi premarital preparation dance was evidently getting farther along in her preparations. Somewhere along the line she must have loosened a catch on the waistband of the minskirt-like garment that was her only item of apparel, because it was slowly sliding over the curves of her well-turned hips, even though her hands remained above her head at all times.

The conga rhythms got more frantic. So did the girl's movements. Her legs were spread wide; yet the minigarment continued to slide farther and farther down. Its upper edge now stood an inch at most above her pubic hair. I had a sneaking suspicion it wouldn't stand there much longer.

I took another look around the room. There still was no sign of Andi Gleason and company. My monocled companion noticed that I was less than enthralled by the goings-on on stage. "Bored?" he asked amiably.

"Not really," I replied. "I just expected something a bit more outré."

He chuckled. "First time here?"

I nodded.

"Be patient. You'll see all you expected and more. I've yet to hear of anyone walking away disappointed. Been coming here myself once a week now for nearly twenty years."

I was about to ask him if, during those twenty years, he had ever come across Andi Gleason and if he had any idea how I might find her, but the conga rhythms had suddenly become so loud that conversation was impossible.

I looked stage-ward to discover that the dancing girl's minigarment had just reached her pubic-hairline. Legs still spread, she began dancing more frantically than ever. At the same time, she gestured toward the minigarment with both hands, as if she were signaling it to slide off her.

Abruptly the congas stopped, and the room fell silent. Simultaneously, the girl brought her legs together and threw her arms over her head. The minigarment fell to her ankles, and she stood totally nude, one knee thrust forward in a pose that invited attention to the sweat-glistened bronze beauty of her splendid thighs, belly and womanhood. She stood still for a moment, then slowly turned a complete circle, giving everyone in the room a three-hundred-and-sixty-degree view of her loveliness. There was polite applause, then it died down, and the girl lowered herself into a supplicant posture, one leg stretched straight forward, the other curled up under her buttocks, her torso bent completely over the axis of the first leg.

The conga players began a soft roll. The three girls who had been squatting in a circle around the featured dancer scurried down the runways and out of sight. I turned to my monocled tablemate. "What happens now?" I asked.

I got my answer from the offstage microphoned voice. "Ladies and gentlemen," he announced, "we have just observed the Bantusi maiden offer her virginity to the sun-god. Now it is time for the crucial part of the premarital preparation ritual. So as to be ready to receive her husband in their marital bed, she will surrender her virginity to the wooden phallus which the Bantusi believe is the sun-god's earthly representative. This is a ritual invented by the Bantusi in the fourteenth century, and still practiced among them today."

I knew the ritual he was talking about. Actually it wasn't of Bantusi origin, and so far as any anthropological studies had ever disclosed, it was not now and never had been practiced by them. It was first described by the Greek historian, Herodotus, who wrote in the fifth century B.C. He claimed that it was practice among the Babylonians. Subsequent studies indicate that it also was practiced by certain tribes of North American Indians, and while there is less than total agreement among scholars who specialize in ancient South American civilizations, many of these scholars believe it was also practiced by the Mayas.

But I wasn't about to voice any objections to the emcee's distortions of historical fact. I had never actually seen the ritual performed, and, even if it was being presented under false colors, I was sure that the performance would be interesting.

It was. Once the emcee's spiel was over, the conga players started in with a rhythm strikingly similar to the contemporary samba. Then two of the girls who had exited earlier returned carrying long, gauze-like white veils, and the third returned with a huge and beautifully carved facsimile of a human penis and testicles.

The instrument was all of thirteen or fourteen inches long, and a good eight inches in circumference. Except for its size, it was extremely lifelike. I was close enough to the stage that I could see the tiniest details. Every muscle, vein and pore of the human organ were faithfully reproduced.

The nude Bantusi maiden who was to submit to the ritual devirgination had remained in her supplicant posture throughout all the comings and goings. Now she stood and retreated to a corner of the stage, from which position she

55

watched with seemingly keen interest the preparations being made by the other three girls.

The girl who was carrying the facsimile phallus brought the object to the center of the stage and, after doing a little dance with it, rested it on its base. Evidently there was considerable weight in the base, because the device stood perfectly upright on its own.

The girls with the veils now did their dance, swirling the material around the phallus as if trying to bring it to a greater state of arousal. The dance culminated with their wrapping the veils around the instrument's testicles, upon the accomplishment of which they retreated to the sidelines. The girl who had carried out the phallus then knelt in front of it and gently caressed its tip with her bare breasts. While she did so, she chanted what presumably was supposed to pass for a Bantusi prayer—and for all I know, it may very well have been.

"The purpose of the veils," explained the offstage microphoned voice, "is to receive the Bantusi maiden's hymenal blood—proof of her virginity. If blood does not flow, the maiden's prospective husband will know that she is not a virgin. She then will be banished from the tribe and sent out into the jungle, where she will be at the mercy of the vicious beasts who inhabit Bantusi-land. The girl who now is praying to the phallus is imploring the sun-god to make the maiden's blood flow freely, so that there will be no doubt in the prospective bridegroom's mind that the maiden is the virgin she claims to be."

All this, of course, was pure hogwash. The Bantusis never practiced this twist, and neither did the Babylonians, the North American Indians or the Mayas. But if the management of The Safari Club didn't know much about anthropology, they certainly knew the tastes of their audience. The announcement was greeted by a delighted squeal from the few females in the audience and by approving grunts and murmurs on the part of the older men.

"I told you you wouldn't be disappointed," my monocled tablemate reminded me. "This is one of the most exciting acts you'll ever see. They perform it here only once or twice a year at most."

I again was about to ask him about Andi Gleason, but once again the congas made conversation impossible. The two drumbeaters, their bodies dripping sweat, set up a polyrhythmic racket that could've raised the dead. In reply,

56

the nude Bantusi maiden started dancing toward the phallus, her body a storm of motion. The other three girls fell into place behind her, matching her movements with her own, as if they both were egging her on and were attempting to share symbolically in her sacrifice.

The conga beating grew even more frantic, and the movements of the four girls took on a proportionate intensity. The maiden gestured with her body toward the phallus, as though she were trying to seduce it. Her acolytes imitated her every gesture, and the total effect was electrifying.

The congas stopped suddenly. The three acolytes again retreated to the wings, and the maiden approached the implement upon which she was to be impaled. The room was so quiet that I could hear the girl's footsteps as she padded barefoot across the stage.

She knelt in front of the phallus and kissed its tip. Then, slowly and almost lovingly, she began licking its glans and stem. The audience was excited to fever pitch. Through the corner of my eye I could see my monocled companion. His hands were both in his lap. In one he held a white handkerchief. With the other he was masturbating.

The maiden stopped kissing the phallus and began caressing it with her breasts. At the same time, she murmured what was either a Bantusi prayer or a nonsense-syllable facsimile of one. Then, ever so slowly, she stood and straddled the huge instrument. The audience's breath was collectively bated as she squatted over it and maneuvered its tip into place against her vulva.

The girl's face took on a pained expression as an inch of the immense organ disappeared inside her. Her entire body quivered, and she appeared to be genuinely frightened. Her three acolytes encouraged her with lusty shouts. She bore down harder, and another inch or two of the organ disappeared.

I watched, fascinated, as she struggled to take even more of the instrument inside her. I found it hard to believe that she actually was a virgin. But, if she wasn't, she was doing an acting job comparable to any I'd ever witnessed.

Clutching the stem of the organ with both hands, she began moving it gently back and forth, as if to widen the channel it was to navigate. Her expression grew more pained. The shouts of her acolytes became more lusty, and the audience began echoing them.

She bore down harder still. Another inch of the instrument

57

disappeared. I found myself holding my breath, as if I were sharing the pain she appeared to be suffering. Rivulets of perspiration dripped from her forehead and limbs, and her wide mouth was twisted into an agonized grimace.

The acolytes began beating rhythmically on the floor with their fists. The congas took up the rhythm, and much of the audience joined in, clapping in tempo. The maiden was motionless for a moment. Then she began rocking in time with the others.

"Boa-a!" the acolytes began chanting with each beat of their fists. "Boa-a! Boa-a!" The audience joined in the chant.

Her face turned skyward, her hands still clutching the pillar on which she was being impaled, her body still rocking in time with the chant, the maiden let out a half-moan, half-scream that soon became a weird hymn. The words, if they were words and not just nonsense syllables, seemed to be a plea to the sun-god for help.

The hymn lasted for perhaps half a minute. Then, eyes squeezed resolutely shut, the girl threw her hands over her head and let her hips sink to the floor. The phallus was immersed to the hilt.

The audience roared its appreciation, but the maiden, if she was aware that she had an audience, gave no sign of it. Her expression now one of ecstasy, she joined her hands over her head in a prayerful festure, and the three acolytes hurried to her side. Clutching her by the waist and arms, they slowly lifted her off the phallus. Then, while two of them ushered her to a corner of the stage, the third displayed the white veils which had been wrapped around the instrument's testicles. Sure enough, the veils were soaked with red.

I couldn't believe that the girl's blood had actually been shed. My guess was that she had been holding some sort of capsule in her hand, and that she had broken it as she took the phallus entirely inside her. But even if it was only a trick, it was a good trick, and the audience knew it. The throngs at Nero's Colosseum couldn't have been more enthusiastic in their cheers when the Christians were fed to the lions.

As the girl with the red-drenched white veils scampered down one of the runways, the lights went out. There was a soft conga roll. Then the emcee's voice intoned, "Ladies and gentlemen, as the climax of this Bantusi ritual, the nubile maiden will receive her husband in their bridal bed."

A moment passed and the lights went back on. One of the conga players had now joined the maiden and her remaining two acolytes on stage, and the artificial phallus had been taken away. While the two acolytes ushered the maiden back to center stage, the conga player peeled off his loincloth. A gasp went up among the females in the audience and a few ribald shouts were supplied by some of the males. Though totally flaccid, the conga player's penis was not much smaller than the wooden instrument on which his bride had just been impaled.

The maiden lay on her back, her legs spread wide. The conga player strode around her, as if inspecting her. Finally he stood between her legs, but facing away from her, and gestured authoritatively toward one of the acolytes. She promptly dropped to her knees in front of him and took his penis in her mouth.

It was at this point that the intended climax of the Bantusi ritual became something of an anti-climax. Whether because of exhaustion, lack of interest or just nervousness about having to perform before so many people, the poor guy just couldn't rise to the occasion. The acolyte worked him over as best she could, but none of her ministrations could produce an erection.

The guy pretended that it was all part of the act. Roughly kicking his hard-working fellatrice away, he barked a few harsh words in Bantusi and summoned the other acolyte. She dutifully bent to the task, and, as an added attraction, massaged the cleft between his buttocks. But that didn't get his motor running either.

The audience grew restless, and I with them. I turned to my monocled companion, figuring that this was as good a time as any to pop my question about Andi Gleason. Unfortunately there was no one there to pop the question to. Somewhere along the line, he had vacated the premises, perhaps for a quick trip to the bathroom.

I looked around the room once again, hoping I might spot Andi or one of the others whose photos I had studied. At first I saw no one whose face looked even vaguely familiar. Then I did saw a lean, hawk-nosed guy who looked very much like a pimp whose mugshot had been part of Andi's dossier. He was sitting at a table near the maître d's desk, accompanied by a tall blonde with a Harpo Marx hairdo and a well-dressed man of sixty who was eyeing the blonde like a buzzard eyes a newly dead carcass.

I was sure that neither the blonde nor the older gent had been represented in Walrus-moustache's photo file. But I was sixty percent sure that the hawk-nose was the pimp whose photo I'd studied. I wanted to make a beeline for him right then and there, but I figured the move would be too risky. So I decided to wait until the show was over and make my play then.

After giving the room another once-over in search of additional familiar faces, none of which was to be found, I tuned in again on the stage action. By this time the conga player had managed to hoist his standard to half mast. Evidently he didn't dare risk suffering a reverse by going for broke, because he quickly shoved his second fellatrice away and leaped into place atop the still-supine maiden. She received him with open thighs, and the two of them pumped away vigorously for a minute or so. Then, forcing what was supposed to pass as a grin of triumph, he got up off her and trotted down the runway and out of sight. I'd've bet my bottom dollar that he hadn't come. The climax, as I said, was anticlimactic.

"Ladies and gentlemen," the offstage emcee said, his voice no longer as confident as it had previously been, "you have just witnessed the famous Bantusi marriage rite. In a few minutes, you will observe an even more exciting spectacle: the sacrifice of a captive white maiden to the chief of the Nairobi tribe. First, however, there will be a brief intermission."

The house lights went on and the waiters descended on the tables like a swarm of bees. I quickly slipped out of my seat and made my way through the crowd toward the table where I had spotted the familiar-looking hawk-nose, but he and his two companions had left their table at the same time that I had left mine. By the time I got to where they had been, they had gone through the street door. I dashed out after them, but I wasn't quick enough. I looked carefully up and down the street and even investigated the alley which began a few buildings away from the club. Neither Hawk-nose nor his pals were anywhere in sight.

Dejected beyond belief, I started back inside the club. "Looking for someone, sir?" the doorman asked me.

"Yeah," I said, mentally kicking myself in the pants for not having questioned him before I went looking. "A skinny guy in his thirties with a tall blonde and another guy."

His eyes stared off into the distance, as if he was racking his brain for any memory of someone who might fit that description. "A thin gentleman, you say?" he mused. "And a tall blonde woman, accompanied by another gentleman, this one a bit older, perhaps in his late fifties?"

"Right!" I beamed. "Which way did they go?"

He smiled cryptically. "Sorry, sir, I can't say I recall seeing anyone who matches that description."

"But they came out right before I did. And you just said——"

"Nossir, can't say I recall anyone who matches that description." His smile broadened and he greeted me with an outstretched palm. "Now, if you took it upon yourself to refresh my memory . . ." He let the sentence trail off.

I got the message. Thrusting a ten shilling note into his hand, I snapped, "Where did they go?"

His eyes took on another far-away look. "Can't say I know, sir. Don't believe they made any mention of where they were going."

"But you did see them."

"That I did. Hailed a cab for them just a few seconds ago. They headed down that way." He pointed to the East. "But, of course, all cabs do, this being a one-way street."

I gripped his arm. "Look, pal, let's stop playing games. It's very important to me that I find them, and I'll make it worth your while if you help me. Now tell me everything you know about them—who they are, what they do, where I can find them . . ."

"You'll make it worth my while, you say? How worth my while?"

"Ten more shillings."

"Ten, hey? How about a hundred?"

I was going to resist, but I remembered that I was on an unlimited expense account from The Coxe Foundation. "Okay, a hundred shillings—five pounds. Now tell me what you know."

He grinned mischievously. "Suppose you let me have the fiver first."

What I wanted to let him have was a fist in the face. But I kept my emotions under control. Stuffing a five-pound note into his hand, I said, "Let's hear it."

His face took on a studious expression. "The elderly gentleman I can't tell you much about. Never saw him until a week ago, and never saw him again before tonight. Both times he was in the company of the younger gentleman. The lady's first name is Melissa. Her last name I don't know. She's something of a newcomer here too. Only saw her once before and don't know anything about her."

"What about the young guy."

"Him I know. Name's Peter Blaine. Comes here quite a bit. Nice chap. A bit quick-tempered, somewhat like yourself, but on the whole a pretty agreeable sort."

"Where can I find him?"

"Can't say I rightly know, seeing as how he just rode off in a cab with the other two for points unknown."

"I mean," I said impatiently, "where can I find him later?"

"Can't say I know that, either. Fellow of irregular habits, Mr. Blaine is. Quite a bit later, though, you might try his apartment."

"Do you know where it is?"

"I do."

"Well, for goodness' sake, man, where?"

He drew a stack of business cards from inside his coat and dealt one off the top. "Here you go, governor. Address, telephone number and all. He has an answering service, by the way, in case you care to leave a message."

I looked at the card. It was one of those costly engraved jobs, and it stated simply: "Peter Blaine, 14 Williamson Mews, London W1, Telephone Regent 7711."

"Pretty fancy calling card for a pimp," I mused under my breath.

"Now, now, guv," admonished the doorman, "no disparaging remarks, if you please. As the saying goes, let the gent who's without sin roll the first stone."

"Well, just for the record, pimping *is* Mr. Blaine's business, isn't it?" I winked conspiratorially. "I mean, I'd hate to chase him all over London only to find that he couldn't set me up with what I'm looking for."

"No worry on that count, guv. He'll set you up with anything your heart desires." He lowered his voice. "Meanwhile, of course, there's always the possibility that it may take you a day or two to get hold of him. And when a gent feels the urge, so to speak, he doesn't always feel like waiting a day or two to satisfy it, if you get what I mean. Now, if I might be of any assistance . . ."

He let the sentence trail off.

"You just might," I said, suddenly aware that this·conniving character could be infinitely more useful to me than Peter Blaine. "I'm looking for a girl named Andi Gleason. Ever hear of her?"

He nodded. "Certainly have."

"Do you know where I can find her?"

"Certainly do."

"For goodness' sake, man, where?"

I got a repeat on the outstretched palm routine. I replied with another five-pound note.

"Well, guv," he smiled, "here's what you do. You go back inside the club, and you sit at your table. Then you look up at the stage. And"—he glanced at his watch—"in about a minute or two, that's where she'll be."

"You mean she's performing here? Tonight?"

"Couldn't've put it more succinctly myself, guv."

"I was told that she quit."

"Matter of fact, she did."

"But now she's back on the job?"

"Matter of fact, she is."

"I want to meet her—personally." I winked to give the "personally" emphasis. "How're my chances?"

"Matter of fact, pretty good."

"Well, earn your five pounds, man. How do I go about it?"

"Send a message backstage with one of the waiters. Give the waiter a fiver for himself and another fiver for Miss Gleason. Then wait. You won't have to wait too long."

I grinned. After all the hassles I'd suffered thanks to the Law of Averages, I was about to get my bone—in the form of Andi Gleason.

CHAPTER FIVE

"Ladies and gentlemen," announced the emcee of The Safari Club, "we now bring you a spectacle of African folklore unsurpassed in literature and the arts. As is well known by anthropologists, certain tribes in Africa's Nairobi region equate beauty with fairness of skin. One of these tribes, the Angustani, has the tradition of presenting to its chief, for his sexual amusement, an annual birthday present of the most fair-skinned maiden that can be found. All year the Angustani prowl the jungles for white women—some who have come to Africa as nurses, others as members of hunting expeditions. When a beautiful white woman is captured, she is held prisoner until the evening of the chief's birthday. Then, in a ceremony which now will be reproduced on our stage, she is offered to the chief."

The lights went out, and a spotlight picked up a bare-breasted Negress on one of the runways. She was one of the three acolytes in the previous spectacle. She carried a censer which emitted puffs of incense as she swung it before her, making her way down the runway and to the center of the stage.

She was followed by two more girls, also holdovers from the previous act. They walked backwards, carrying beautiful white feathers all of four feet long, with which they fanned the path behind them.

The feather-girls were followed by a tall, black-skinned man—the conga player who had remained offstage while his partner played husband to the Bantusi maiden in the previous act. He wore white silk pantaloons, a white silk turban with an enormous false gem over his forehead, and a chain of shark's teeth around his neck. He was followed by the erstwhile Bantusi maiden, who swung another incense-puffing censer.

The blatant falseness of the spectacle amused me. There was, of course, absolutely no evidence, anthropological or otherwise, that any Nairobi tribes subscribed to a tradition of gifting its chief annually with a fair-skinned sexmate. There was, in fact, no tribe known as the Angustani—obviously a made-up name, more Indian than African—and even if there had been, the tribesmen couldn't well prowl the jungles for white captives; Nairobi was a desert region, and the nearest jungle was hundreds of miles away. Incense was of European and Oriental origin, not African, and the Nairobis almost certainly never had heard of it. The feathers were a Pakistani touch, and the pseudo-Nairobi chief's costuming was more Saudi Arabian than anything else.

But this melange of phony touches didn't seem to bother the audience, to whom the play evidently was the thing. And The Safari Club players, probably West Indian immigrants, went through the motions of their ludicrous charade with all the solemnity of Hollywood extras doing the Cecil B. deMille thing.

When the pantalooned pseudo-chief reached center-stage, he lowered himself regally into a thronelike wooden chair. The two feather-bearers positioned themselves at his flanks, dutifully continuing to fan him. The incense-girls sat cross-legged at his feet, their censers sending up clouds of sweet-smelling smoke.

The chief then clapped his hands twice, whereupon another dark-skinned man—the conga player who, last time around, had had such a hard time getting his equipment in working order—materialized on the runway. He was clad only in a loincloth and was shouldering a silver platter, much in the same manner that a waiter shoulders a tray of dishes. On the platter, decked out in a billowy, gauze-thin green gown, was none other than Andi Gleason.

It was time for me to do another of my double-takes. Having seen the photos of her in Walrus-moustache's dossier, I had expected to find a beautiful young partygirl, perhaps frayed a bit at the edges as partygirls are wont to become very early in their careers, but nonetheless eminently appealing and appetizing.

The Andi Gleason now being served up to The Safari Club's black pseudo-chief was neither appealing nor appetizing—nor young. I guessed her age at twenty-seven or twenty-eight, which isn't terribly old, even for a partygirl. But the toll which her years on the circuit had taken of her was considerable.

Her face wore the beaten look of a Charles Street B-girl at five o'clock Sunday morning. Her eyes sported more crows-feet than any five aviaries, and her heavy make-up called attention to them rather than disguised them. Her mouth was a thin, expressionless pencil-line of bored detachment.

Her body had once been very good—the breasts small but provocative, the legs long and lithe, the curves clean and sexy. But too many years of too much booze and drugs, and too little sleep, had aged her prematurely. Her muscle tone was shot, and her spine had surrendered to a perpetual slump. She had defeat written all over her in capital letters.

I marveled that she had looked so good in her photographs. But then, cameras have been known to lie—or at least to bend the truth a little. What was more remarkable was that an M.P. like Christopher Smythe, who obviously could've done better, had managed to get hooked on her. Walrus-mosutache seemed to think drugs or some other persuasive agent was involved. Seeing her in the flesh, I was inclined to agree. One thing was certain: Andi had to be holding Smythe by some means other than her raw sex appeal, which was, to put it charitably, minimal.

When the ex-conga player who was carrying her on his silver platter reached center-stage, he knelt in front of the pseudo-chief's throne. Andi then stepped tiredly off the platter and stood waiting for someone to tell her what to do next. She looked dazed, and I was willing to bet that she'd prepared herself for the evening's performance by getting stoned on marijuana or something stronger.

The pseudo-chief got up and began pacing around her, as if inspecting the merchandise. He opened her gown, tweaked her breast experimentally, then gave her buttocks a pinch. She continued to stare dazedly ahead, as if totally oblivious to his ministrations. The other man and the four Negro girls exchanged nervous glances. Obviously Andi wasn't playing her part the way it was supposed to be played.

The pseudo-chief paced some more. Then he ripped the gown off Andi's back and gave her a resounding slap on the buttocks. She jumped slightly, and said, "Ow, cut that out!" Then she slipped back into her daze.

The other members of the cast exchanged a few more nervous glances. The pseudo-chief paced some more, seemingly at a loss. Finally he turned to the platter-bearer. "The girl act funny," he said, adding to the evening's store of anachronisms the spectacle of a Nairobi chief who spoke English—with a Jamaican accent, yet. "She don't seem afraid."

"She very afraid earlier," replied the platter-bearer. "I give her leafs from peyote plant to calm her down."

The audience obviously sensed that something was amiss. There were murmurs of disapproval, accompanied by the shuffling of feet. "Me no like calm woman," ad-libbed the pseudo-chief. "Me like lively woman."

"Me sorry," apologized his partner. "Me no think peyote leafs make her this calm."

The audience grew more restive. The murmurs increased in volume and two or three men began calling out loud for a new girl. My monocled tablemate, now back on the scene, whispered, "Something is wrong. The girl is supposed to be fighting, and the men aren't supposed to be talking."

The pseudo-chief paced some more. After a moment he evidently had an inspiration. "Me wake her up," he grinned. "Me show her how to be lively woman." Seizing her roughly by the arm, he tipped her over his knee and began to administer a vigorous spanking.

The first few blows failed to disturb Andi's drug-induced torpor. But the next few made her squirm, and the few after that—sharp, resounding blows that echoed throughout the

66

room—really got her moving. Her arms and legs began flailing wildly about. "Stop it, for Chrissakes!" she yelled. "What the hell's the matter with you?"

The pseudo-chief, grinning, hit her all the harder. Her creamy white buttocks took on a bright pink glow. He hit her some more. The pink rapidly turned to red.

"Hey!" Andi was screaming. "Lay off, will ya, ya stupid spook! What're ya tryin' a do!?"

The audience roared its approval, and the audience's reaction—combined, perhaps, with a few sadistic leanings of his own—inspired the pseudo-chief to new heights of energy. He swung harder and harder still, and the more fiercely Andi struggled to escape the blows, the more energetically he administered them.

The spanking lasted for all of two or three minutes, by which time Andi's bottom had already begun to turn black and blue. The pseudo-chief then dumped her roughly onto the floor, tore open his pantaloons, and, brandishing proudly the proof of his masculine prowess, proceeded to rape her.

It was a genuine rape, because Andi by this time had had her fill of the game and was fighting desperately to resist his advances. But he was much too strong for her, and her resistance served only to prolong her agony. I watched the spectacle with a feeling of pity and disgust. But the audience obviously loved every minute of it. They had expected only a pretended rape, and now they were getting the real thing. They couldn't have been happier.

I had little doubt that many of the members of this audience were the same people who supported publicly The Big Prig's campaign against the free dissemination of erotic literature. I was sure that a few of them were sincerely convinced that the sexual permissiveness of England's young people was proof positive that the Empire was in a state of decay. Yet here they were, these same pompous hypocrites, enjoying amidst the posh surroundings of The Safari Club perverted sexual pleasures that the young people they condemned would never think of. It was enough to turn one's stomach.

But I didn't have time to wallow in my righteous indignation, because, while I was fuming inside at the spectacle I was witnessing and the audience that was applauding it, the rape scene ended and Andi Gleason was spirited off the stage. I didn't want to risk letting her get away before I had a chance to talk with her. Discarding as too time-consuming the ploy which the doorman had suggested as my best way of meeting

67

her, I slipped out of my seat, collared the nearest waiter, stuffed a pair of five-pound notes into his hand and said, "Take me to the white girl's dressing room."

He took one look at my tip, which amounted to almost twenty-five dollars in American money, and gulped. "Come with me."

Andi's dressing room was the dressing room for the entire cast. They were all there when the waiter ushered me in, and none of them seemed to find my presence noteworthy. The two men, who were changing into their costumes for the next spectacle, were being railed at by Andi. They were chuckling amusedly at her furor.

"I'm telling you, Eddie," she was saying to the erstwhile pseudo-chief, "you ever pull a stunt like that again and you'll be sorry."

"You learn how to keep your head when you're working," Eddie replied, "and I won't have to pull any stunts."

The waiter told her I wanted to speak to her. It took a few seconds for the message to work its way through her angry and drug-clouded brain. When it registered, she regarded me with a dazed expression. "Whattaya want, Jack?" she asked.

I got right to the point. Peeling half a dozen five-pound notes off the roll Walrus-moustache had supplied me with, I laid them out on the dressing table in front of her. "I want you," I said.

She looked at the notes, then at me, then back at the notes.

"I ain't workin' tonight, Jack," she said after a moment.

I added another thirty pounds to the thirty already on the table. "That's sixty pounds," I reminded her. "I'm told you usually go for ten."

"Sixty pounds!" exclaimed the pseudo-chief. "You ain't gonna get many more offers like that, Andi."

One of the black girls sidled up to me. "If she's not working tonight, mister, I am."

"I want her," I said.

Andi touched the money, as if to reassure herself that it was actually there. "I don't do no kinky stuff, Jack, if that's what you have in mind," she said.

"No kinky stuff," I said. "Just straight sex."

She picked up the bills, counted them, then held them in her hand as if she didn't know quite what to do next with them. "Oh, wow," she murmured after a moment. "Sixty pounds. You gotta be kidding."

I said nothing.

"Well, okay," she said finally. "I'll go with you. But it's gotta be fast. I got another show to do two hours from now, and my boss don't like it if I'm late."

"I want you for the whole night," I told her.

"No good. I don't go for the whole night."

"Not even for a hundred pounds?" Even though The Coxe Foundation was footing the bill, I found my extravagance hard to believe.

"I don't go the whole night," she said.

From outside the dressing room I could hear the emcee announcing the evening's next spectacle—a girl who would perform a variety of sex acts with a Great Dane. The girl was another white girl, who had been sitting in one corner of the room petting her prospective sex-partner. One of the Negro men ushered her out on the runway. The other man and the four girls, tossing trenchcoats over their costumes, filed out the back door, apparently for a breath of air.

"Look," I said to Andi now that we were alone, "I really want to spend the night with you. Don't tell me you never go for the whole night, because I know guys you've gone with."

She glanced around, as if to make sure no one would overhear us. Her eyes had a faraway look that said she was still feeling her drugs, but she seemed to be gaining control of herself. "What's your act, Jack?" she asked. "Why do you want me?"

I smiled. "I like you."

"A hundred pounds worth?"

"Yeah, a hundred pounds worth. Maybe more, if you're as good as I think you're going to be."

She seemed to be wondering whether or not to believe me. For all of thirty seconds she didn't answer. Then slowly the corners of her mouth arched upward in a small smile. The smile said that, monetary considerations aside, she dug me. "I can't go the whole night with you," she said. "But I'll go with you now. We can have an hour or so together, if you want."

I decided not to press my luck. "Come on," I told her, reaching for her hand. "My hotel's just a couple blocks away."

She drew away from me. "I can't leave with you. Tell me where to go, and I'll meet you there."

I smirked. "You don't expect me to fall for that old routine, do you, honey?"

She frowned. "Don't you trust me?"

"I trust everybody, but I always cut the cards anyway."

The metaphor escaped her, but the message didn't. She

69

handed me back my sixty pounds. "Take your money, Jack. Pay me when I get there."

I couldn't be sure that she'd actually come. But I had the feeling that I'd never be able to persuade her to accept any other arrangement. "Okay, here's the address," I said, scribbling my room number and the name and address of the hotel on a slip of paper. "Try not to take too long."

"I won't," she promised.

I went back to my table, where I signaled the waiter for my check. My monocled tablemate looked at me with surprise. "Leaving so soon?" he asked.

I nodded. "Got a pressing appointment."

He gestured toward the stage, where the girl who did the dog act was giving her canine companion a few preliminary caresses. "This is the best part of the show. She and the dog actually make love."

"Sorry," I smiled. "I'll see it some other time." I paid the waiter and headed for the door. The look the monocled gent gave me told me he thought I ought to have my head examined.

Back at the Eros, I poured myself a Johnnie Walker Black, kicked off my shoes and flopped down on the bed. While I waited for Andi Gleason I wondered what pressing reason she had for not wanting to spend the night with me—a reason so pressing that she had turned down the equivalent of two hundred and fifty American dollars, and the possibility of earning more.

Did she have a date after work with another man? Christopher Smythe, for example?

It was possible, but not likely. Smythe, indiscreet though he might have been in his affair with her, still had *some* appearances to maintain. He was still living with his wife and children, and he was due on the floor of the House of Commons at nine in the morning. I doubted that he'd abandon discretion entirely and go galavanting around London with his paramour in the wee small hours of the ayem. Probably he saw Andi only on weekends, and occasionally for midweek afternoon quickies when he could safely break away.

But if her date wasn't Smythe, who was he? Maybe some John who was going to pay her more than I had offered?

Again, possible—but damned unlikely. In the shape Andi Gleason was in, ten pounds was a lot of money for an all-night shot. Any John who'd pay more had to be interested in more than just sex. And what more did she have to offer?

70

If she was actually setting up Smythe for a Commie squeeze play, she had a lot to offer to anyone working for the other side. But the other side consisted of the British Secret Service and The Coxe Foundation. According to Walrus-moustache, the British Secret Service had decided to let The Coxe Foundation handle the whole show. And for the present, I *was* The Coxe Foundation. So she really didn't have anything to offer to anybody except me.

Another possibility, of course, was that she had to meet one of her Commie contacts after work. But now that I thought of it, if she was on the Commie team, what was she doing working at The Safari Club in the first place? The Commies don't make a practice of leaving their operatives out in the open where people like me and the boys from the British Secret Service can get to them, unless there's a damned good reason for it. I could think of no reason why they'd want anyone to get to Andi at this stage of the game, but I could think of a lot of reasons why they wouldn't.

Also, if she was working for the Commies, how did it happen that she was stoned out of her mind on pot—or whatever it was that she was stoned on? People who aren't in full control of their faculties are lousy security risks. The Communists don't take chances with lousy security risks.

So maybe she wasn't working for the Communists after all.

But, if she wasn't, who was she working for?

The Friends of Decency? I'd already reasoned my way out of that possibility.

And, if not the Friends, who else?

There didn't seem to be any other candidates.

In any case, it was my job to get her out of England as soon as I could. And that, judging from what I'd seen so far, wasn't going to be an easy task.

I'd match my sexual abilities with any man's, and I'd venture to say that I could make a lot of girls fall madly enough in love with me that they'd consent to slipping off somewhere for a month or two of uninterrupted love-making.

But love and sex are a lure only to girls who are emotionally and sexually responsive. Unless I missed my guess, Andi Gleason was so heavily into the drug scene that she had lost the ability to respond.

So, if I couldn't get to her via love and sex, how could I get to her?

Come to think of it, would I ever get the chance to get to her? Fifteen minutes had gone by since I left her at The

Safari Club. The Eros Hotel was only a five-minute walk away. Where the hell was she?

I polished off my Johnnie Walker Black and poured myself another one. Five more minutes passed and Andi still hadn't made the scene.

Ten minutes later, while I was wondering whether to go back to The Safari Club looking for her, she showed up. I needed only one look at her eyes to realize that she'd paused en route for another whack at whatever it was that had her whacked out. She stared through me, smiled giddily, tossed me a vacuous "Hi, Jack," staggered across the room, and passed out on the bed. I knew better than to try arousing her. Demon pot, or whatever, had done its job too well.

I sat in the chair next to the bed and, staring idly at the unconscious body beside me, entertained a few negative thoughts about the proliferation of marijuana and other consciousness-altering agents in contemporary society.

Andi Gleason was out for all of three hours. I was dozing when she came to, and I woke up to find her giggling uproariously while staring at her fingernails.

"What's so funny?" I asked.

She giggled some more, then, not looking at me, said simply, "It's a gas."

Andi amused herself with her fingernails for another three or four minutes. Then, as if noticing me for the first time, she smiled. "Hi, Jack."

"Hi," I replied dully.

These amenities having been exchanged, she lay down and went back to sleep.

She woke an hour later. I'd undressed for bed by this time, and my pajamas evidently reminded her that I'd engaged her for sexual purposes.

"Sixty pounds," she said, more to herself than to me. "Who'd ever think anybody'd pay me sixty pounds?"

When I didn't reply, she began undressing. She seemed surprised that I still had my pajamas on when she had stripped to the altogether.

"Well, where's the sixty pounds, Jack?" she asked, a trace of impatience in her voice. "I ain't doing anything until I get paid."

I gave her the sixty pounds. Actually I didn't feel like doing anything but booting her out of the room and calling it a night. But I knew I might not get another crack at her for a while, and I had to make the best of the crack I had. She'd already overstayed the two-hour break before her next scheduled performance at The Safari Club, and my only hope was to figure out some way to keep her with me until she came down from her high and was able to converse coherently.

She took the money, fumbled around with it for a moment as if searching her nude body for a pocket to put it in, giggled at her forgetfulness, then spotted her purse on the dresser, stumbled over to it, and put the money inside. "Well," she smiled giddily, throwing her arms over her head like a dancer at the end of a theatrical number, "here I am. Take me."

Shucking off my pajamas, I maneuvered her onto the bed. Her legs spread open mechanically, and she received me. I've always thought of myself as pretty all-right in the size department, but this time I'd clearly met my match. I felt like a row-boat navigating the Amazon River. Amendment: like a camel navigating the Sahara Desert. Rivers are wet, and Andi was bone-dry.

She flopped around wildly beneath me. Her face was distorted into a silly grin, and she punctuated her movements with sighs, groans and moans of "Oh, Jack!" But it was obviously an act—and not a very convincing one. I would've bet anything that she didn't even feel me inside her.

I tried my best to put some zing into things. But it wasn't easy. I'd always maintained that sex is like business: when it's good, it's very very good, and when it's bad, it's still pretty good. In Andi Gleason I found an exception to the case. Fortunately I'm a priapist, or I'd've surely lost my impetus mid-way through the first stroke.

Still, I had to keep her with me, and the only way I could think of doing it was to make our sex act last as long as possible. Entertaining all sorts of delicious fantasies involving other girls I'd bedded down with, I forced myself to continue. I couldn't remember ever enjoying the mating game less. Stoically, I resolved that I'd hang on until she came down from her high or until exhaustion did me in.

Thankfully, I didn't have to hang on much longer. After about ten minutes of squirming and sighing, groaning and moaning, she passed out again. Relieved, I dismounted, slipped under the covers and went to sleep. I wrapped one arm around hers to make sure I'd wake up whenever she did.

She woke three hours later. Dawn's first shafts of light were filtering through the heavily curtained window opposite the bed, and somewhere not too far away Big Ben was tolling six. Andi sat up in bed, rubbed her eyes, and looked bewilderedly around the room. Then she turned to me as if seeing me for the first time.

"Wow," she said, "what a trip." Almost as an afterthought she added, "Who are you?"

"The guy you balled last night. Remember?"

Her face took on a thoughtful expression, as though she were trying to see through the haze of her high and piece together the events leading up to the present. Suddenly her expression became one of alarm. "Jeez, I missed the last two shows!" She started to get up, as if by really hustling she could make up for lost time. Then, realizing that she couldn't, she abandoned the effort and got back into bed. "Jeez, Mr. Guy-I-Balled-Last-Night, I'm in trouble."

I put on my best bedside manner. "What kind of trouble, hon?"

"Big trouble."

For a moment, it looked like she was going to elaborate. Then the wheels inside her head evidently began turning in a different direction. "You wouldn't want to hear about it," she said, pecking me lightly on the cheek. Then she got up and began searching for her clothes.

"I would want to hear about it," I said. "Suppose you tell me."

She found her panties and climbed into them. "Nah, the whole thing's a drag. It depresses me just to think about it."

"Maybe you'd be less depressed if you got it off your chest."

She flashed an obviously insincere smile that was designed to tell me to mind my own business. "Thanks anyway, Jack," she said, putting on her bra. "I think I'll just keep it to myself for now."

I got out of bed and shoveled two scoops of coffee into the electric percolator with which the management of the Eros had thoughtfully equipped my room. I was pretty sure I wasn't going to get her to talk unless I tried something pretty dramatic. So I tried something pretty dramatic. "How's my friend, Christopher Smythe?" I asked.

She almost managed to cover up her shocked reaction to the question. Almost, but not quite. She put on an expression of bewilderment, but not before I got a glimpse of the astonishment in her eyes when I mentioned Smythe's name. "Smythe?" she replied, feigning nonchalance. "Don't think I

74

know him. Does he hang around The Safari Club?"

I let my grin tell her that I saw through her act. "He hangs around the House of Commons, mostly. And you know him pretty damned well. Now what do you say we talk about the trouble you're in."

To avoid looking at me, she tugged her sweater over her head. "You got the wrong girl, Jack," she mumbled from beneath it. "I never been in the House of Commons."

I walked over to where she was. When her face surfaced through the neckhole of the sweater, my face was just inches away from it. I took her jaw between my thumb and fingers, and held her so that she couldn't look away from me. "Andi Gleason," I said through clenched teeth, "you *are* in trouble, and I'm probably the only guy you know who can bail you out. Play ball with me, and I'll pull your chestnuts out of the fire. Don't play ball with me, and I'll throw you to the wolves. Take your pick."

I released her. She looked at me for a moment, as if trying to decide whether to take me up on my offer. Then, turning away, she made a production of looking for her skirt. "I don't know what you're talking about, Jack," she said under her breath.

I went back to the percolator, speaking as I walked. "Andi, you're doing a number on Christopher Smythe, and your girlfriend, Diane Dionne, is doing a number on James Whelan. You thought you had the situation under control for a while, but now everything seems to be falling apart on you. I can help you. All you've got to do is say yes and I'll have you on a plane for the United States quicker than you can say 'God save the queen.' All your expenses will be paid, and you can stay there under police protection until it's safe for you to come back here."

I turned to her and waited for a reaction. There wasn't any. Keeping her head lowered so that I couldn't see her eyes, she busied herself with the zipper on her miniskirt.

"Well?" I prodded. "How about it? You know your thing with Christopher Smythe is falling apart. And you know that when it does you're going to be in worse trouble than you are now. I can bail you out. I'll arrange transportation to the States, police protection, all your expenses and"—an afterthought—"all the drugs you need. Interested?"

She zipped up the miniskirt and put on her shoes. "I don't know what you're talking about, Jack," she murmured, suddenly in a big hurry to get out of the room.

I stood in front of the door to block her way. "You know damned well what I'm talking about. And you're a very foolish girl if you don't take me up on my offer."

"I'm a very foolish girl," she said, her expression now one of impatience. "So let me out of here, will ya? Or do I . . . I . . ." She fumbled around, apparently in search of an appropriate threat. Then she abandoned the attempt. "Who are you, Jack? Why are you so interested in me?"

"I'm a representative of the United States government," I replied. "I'm working hand in hand with the British Secret Service. We know that you and Diane are doing a number on Christopher Smythe and James Whelan. What we don't know is why."

She smiled sardonically. "So you want me to tell you why, right? And then you'll set me up in a rose-covered cottage in San Francisco, just because you think I'm a nice girl." She made another start for the door. "No thanks, Jack. I'll take my chances without you."

I held the door closed behind me. "Don't be foolish, Andi. I'm the only chance you've got."

She tried to force her way past me. Then, realizing she wasn't strong enough, she backed away. "Look, Jack," she said defeatedly, "if you're going to arrest me, go ahead and arrest me. And if you aren't, how's about getting the hell out of the doorway?"

"I want to know what you're trying to do with Christopher Smythe. Some people think you're playing ball with the Communists. I don't think so, and I want to find out who you're actually playing ball with."

The mention of the Communists seemed to bewilder and frighten her. I'd only been playing a hunch so far, but her expression told me that my hunch was right on target.

She backed away from me. "I think I'd like a cup of coffee," she said.

I motioned her toward the armchair, then poured two cups from the percolator. "Who are you playing ball with, Andi?"

"Tell me more about that cottage in San Francisco."

I handed her one cup. "I'll get you out of England within twenty-four hours after you say you want to go. You'll have police protection, and all the money you need. All I want from you in return is the complete story about your affair with Christopher Smythe."

"How do I know I won't be arrested?"

I almost asked, "For what?" But I caught myself in time.

76

Following up on my hunch, I said, "You mean for extortion?"

She looked away from me. "I'm not admitting anything just yet."

"I know you're extorting Smythe. But I'm playing for bigger stakes. You see, the Communists know you're extorting Smythe also, and they're trying to beat you to the punch. But they're not just looking for money. They want a lot more. That's why the British Secret Service is interested in you, and that's why I'm interested. Now, tell me, who put you up to it?"

She sipped her coffee. "Look," she said after a moment, "I've got to think about this. I mean I'm all shook up right now, and I need some time to get my head together. I'm scared; I won't deny it. But I've got to have time to think."

"There isn't any time to waste."

She took another sip of coffee, then put the cup on the nighttable and stood up. "I'm getting out of here, Jack," she said suddenly. "I don't think I like you anymore."

Again I blocked the door. "Don't be foolish, Andi. Take the chance while you have it."

"Get out of the way, Jack. I'm tired of playing games."

I sensed that further resistance on my part would only harden her resistance. "Okay, take some time to think. Meet me tonight and we'll talk some more."

"Okay. I'll come over on my first break, just like I did last night."

I smiled. "Promise?"

She smiled back. "No promises. If I decide yes, I'll be here. If I decide no, I won't."

"One thing before you go: if you feel you want to see me before then—if you need my help, or if you want to see me for any reason whatever—call me. My name is Rod Damon. The hotel switchboard will take the message if I'm not in. Let them know where I can find you, and I'll get back to you as soon as I can."

Her smile broadened. "Thanks. I'm beginning to like you again."

"One more thing: I'd like to talk to Diane Dionne. How about introducing me to her?"

She shook her head. "Maybe later. Not now."

I opened the door. She kissed me goodbye before walking through it. Then she waved another goodbye before she turned the corner and started down the hall toward the elevator. I waved back and closed the door. Suddenly, I found myself beginning to like Andi Gleason too.

Back in the room, I took my coffee to the window overlooking the street. Standing there, I made one of the silly little bets I occasionally make with myself. In a minute or two, Andi would walk out the front door of the hotel. According to my bet, if she looked up toward my window as she left, that would mean she'd be back that night ready to tell me all I wanted to know. If she didn't look up, she wouldn't be back and I'd have to find another way of getting to the bottom of the mystery.

A minute passed, then another. Then Andi walked out the door, crossed the street, and headed toward Picadilly Circus. She never so much as glanced toward my window. I hoped against hope that my silly little bet was just a silly little bet and not a valid indication of what to expect. But I had a strange feeling that I had lost both the bet and Andi.

I continued to stare out the window. The street was all but deserted—or had been before she left the hotel. Now, suddenly, it wasn't deserted anymore.

No sooner had she crossed the street than a man came out of the hotel. From my angle, I couldn't see his face. But I got a good look at his clothes. He was wearing evening attire, just as most of the older men at The Safari Club had been the night before.

Keeping about fifty yards behind her, he crossed the street. A black Austin-Healy was parked at the curb. He rapped on the window, which promptly opened. Then he said something to the driver.

Another man now got out of the passenger side of the car—a man wearing a rumpled business suit. He crossed the street and disappeared inside the Eros. The guy in evening clothes started walking after Andi. She turned left at the next block, and he turned left behind her. She seemed to have no idea that he was tailing her. A minute later, the Austin-Healy slowly pulled out of its parking place and joined the parade.

So all of a sudden Andi Gleason was a Very Important Person.

But important to whom? It seemed unlikely that the Friends of Decency would be tailing her.

It seemed even less likely that the British Secret Service would be involved. They had told Walrus-moustache that the Smythe-Whelan affair was our baby, and they'd never been known to reneg on a deal with us.

That narrowed the field down to a single candidate: the Communists. Or was it possible that someone else—someone The Coxe Foundation never suspected of having an interest in the case—was on the scene?

Now that I thought about it, it was very possible. And the list of potential candidates was virtually inexhaustible.

It couldn've been the press. London's newspapers—especially the Sunday sheets like *News of the World* and *The Mirror*—were always on the lookout for a scandal. One or more papers could've got wind of the Smythe-Whelan case, just as the Coxe Foundation had. If so, they'd be sure to have reporters trailing the principals every step of the way.

It could've been the spies of some other nation.—France, for example, or Germany. Everybody in the Western Bloc was supposed to be part of one happy family. But members of even the happiest families sometimes turn against each other, and who could say what sort of strategies were being cooked up behind the closed doors of any of these nations' equivalents of The Coxe Foundation.

It could've been Smythe and Whelan's rivals for office in the upcoming elections. Quite possibly they had heard some rumors and had put a team of investigators on the trail to find out what was what—and to get proof of it.

For that matter, it could've been Smythe and Whelan themselves. The two M.P.'s, obviously enough, were being extorted by Andi and Diane. I had guessed that very early in my conversation with Andi, and her subsequent remarks confirmed the guess. It was entirely possible that the two extortion victims were now trying to drum up some information that would help them get out of the hold Andi and Diane evidently had on them.

Walrus-moustache had suggested that some sort of brainwashing might be involved. But this suggestion had been based on the assumption that the Communists were behind the deal—an assumption now all but proven false.

He had also suggested drugs. But judging from what I'd seen of Andi, she couldn't handle drugs herself, much less use them to manipulate other people.

In any case, Andi and Diane evidently had their hooks firmly into Smythe and Whelan—as evidenced by Smythe and Whelan's refusal to walk out of the affair when they were approached through diplomatic channels by The Coxe Foundation.

And, sure as shooting, the two girls weren't playing the

79

game on their own. Andi's allusions to being in big trouble made this plain enough.

But, if the girls weren't playing the game on their own, who was playing it with them? And what were the stakes?

The stakes, it now seemed, were cash—nothing more, nothing less. I'd first guessed that when I found Andi working at The Safari Club. I could think of no reason why she possibly would've gone back to work there unless she really needed the money—money which she could no longer earn as a prostitute because, perhaps, something or other about her caper with Christopher Smythe made it too dangerous for her to work as a prostie.

I became convinced that my guess was on target when she declined my offer of thirty pounds for a roll in the hay. A down-at-the-heels dame like her didn't rate ten pounds, let alone thirty. And yet she had turned me down cold. Why? Presumably because she had some reason to believe that turning a trick with a John—any John—would jeopardize the Smythe-Whelan caper.

Then I had upped the ante to sixty, and she almost didn't accept even then. When she finally—and reluctantly—did accept, she still nixed the offer of one hundred pounds for an all-night shot. Evidently whoever had masterminded the Smythe-Whelan caper had firmly warned her against turning any tricks, and while she might risk a quickie because she desperately needed the cash, she wouldn't risk an all-nighter.

All this had led me to theorize that she envisioned a big bundle of cash at the end of the rainbow when the Smythe-Whelan caper was over.

So now the question arose: What made Smythe and Whelan such lucrative targets? Fortunately I could get some help answering that one from Walrus-moustache—and I planned to send out my call for help just as soon as I could get to a telephone that I was sure wasn't bugged.

Meanwhile, the old question—the question of who was behind Andi and Diane in the Smythe-Whelan caper—remained. I'd have to answer that all by myself.

I glanced at my watch. It read seven fifteen. I'd been standing at the window for close to twenty minutes, and the guy in the rumpled business suit still hadn't come out of the hotel. Evidently he was going to tail me while his two buddies tailed Andi.

It would've been interesting to play counter-tail with him. I'd been doing the spy thing long enough now that I was pretty sure I could give him the slip once he started following me, then double around and tail him until he finally gave up and returned to whomever it was that had sent him after me. Once I found out, I'd know who was so interested in Andi Gleason—and, if I was lucky, why.

But playing counter-tail might take all day, and I had more important ways to spend my time—like setting up shop for my sex survey at the Big Prig's mansion. Besides, for all I knew, I might just counter-tail the guy back to the Fleet Street offices of one of the Sunday newspapers. There'd be no profit in that.

After shaving and dressing I went down to the hotel's dining room. A hefty plate of wheatcakes and a pot of tea later, I made my way to the lobby. Sure enough, the guy in the rumpled suit was there. He sat in an armchair pretending keen interest in the latest edition of *The Daily Mail*.

I asked the desk for messages, of which I knew there wouldn't be any. Through the corner of my eye, I watched Rumpled Suit. No question about it, he was an expert at his job. He never so much as glanced up from his paper.

I bought a pack of gum from the desk clerk, got a surprised "Thank you, sir!" when I told him to keep the change from a ten-shilling note, then ambled outside. Next door to the Eros was a discount men's clothing store. I ducked into the foyer and pretended to study the window display. Rumpled Suit came strolling out of the hotel, his *Daily Mail* tucked neatly under his arm.

Yep, he was an expert. He didn't look around frantically to see which direction I'd gone off in, as a novice might. Instead, he very casually surveyed the street, as if contemplating what a lovely morning it was. Then, when he didn't see me, he turned nonchalantly to his right and began walking toward Picadilly Circus—the direction, presumably, in which he guessed I'd be most apt to go.

I waited until he was a block away. Then, while he was checking out the intersecting street to see if I had gone down it, I ducked back inside the Eros, slipped the desk clerk a pair of five-pound notes, and asked if anybody had questioned him about me during the course of the night.

He said that nobody had and gave me back the notes. Evidently he didn't consider it cricket to take the money without earning it.

I tucked the bills into his shirt pocket and asked him to tell me all he knew about Rumpled Suit.

This time he kept the money and more than earned it. Rumpled Suit, he reported, had checked into the hotel around three a.m. He was sharing a room with another man, who had checked in about an hour earlier. The first man, who wore evening clothes, had sat in the lobby until about six thirty that morning, then left. Rumpled Suit, meanwhile, had left a few minutes after he checked in, then returned right after Evening Clothes left and had sat in the lobby ever since.

Real experts, these boys were. Checked into the hotel as guests, rather than trying to do a freebie stakeout in the lobby, and never revealed their hand by asking questions about me. But they were up against another expert—namely yours truly, who, with good old American know-how, realized that the best way to get inside info was to grease the right palms. I gave the clerk another ten pounds and asked him not to say anything about me to anyone. Then I headed back outside.

Rumpled Suit was making his way back toward the Eros as I walked out. Ever the expert, he gave no indication that he saw me. I was tempted to bid him good morning, just to let him know I was on to his game. But the dumber he thought I was, the easier it'd be to get the better of him. I passed him without a nod, then hailed a cab to the American Express Office. If there was one place in London where I could be sure I could safely phone Walrus-moustache, that was it.

My Coxeman-in-Chief was not, of course, available at the other end of the telephone cable. But I was sure he'd get the message soon enough. I told the secretary who answered that I wanted a complete financial statement on Christopher Smythe and James Whelan plus all their immediate relatives; also, any newspaper clippings I could get that might relate to their financial activities and/or their social lives; also, any newsclips about the financial doings of anyone else in London or elsewhere named Christopher Smythe or James Whelan, or anyone who might conceivably be mistaken for a relative of the real Smythe or Whelan. I suggested that The Coxe Foundation's London people could dig up most of this data locally, then deliver it to me at the Eros. It was, I knew, a lot of work to put my colleagues through just to satisfy a hunch of mine. But, at this stage of the proceedings, the hunch was all I had to go on, and I needed all the help I could get.

The phone call having been accomplished, I left American Express and hailed a cab for The Big Prig's mansion. As we pulled out from the curb, I noticed a guy who had been standing nonchalantly outside the American Express office pretending great interest in *The Morning Telegram*. I don't know how he had managed to follow me there, but he sure as hell had. It was none other than my old friend, Rumpled Suit.

No doubt about it, he was a ballplayer's ballplayer—a real pro. What a shame we happened to be on opposite teams.

CHAPTER SIX

The rest of the morning passed uneventfully. I spent my time organizing the crew of administrative assistants The Big Prig had placed at my disposal for the proposed study of the connection, if any, between the free dissemination of erotic literature and sexual permissiveness in contemporary London. The crew consisted of frumpy Gretchen Stark, who was its captain, and six girls ranging in age from twenty-two to twenty-five and ranging in appearance from just-plain-unattractive to downright-hideous. I naturally would have preferred a more comely group, but I had to admit that the present situation wasn't without its advantages: at least I was able to keep my mind on my work. I can't recall ever accomplishing so much in such little time.

For lunch I was the guest of Lord and Lady Brice-Bennington. Lord B-B, I found, was a stiff-upper-lip sort who evidently operated under the assumption that table conversation shouldn't involve any topic more controversial than the weather or yesterday's soccer scores. I tried to draw him into a chat about the upcoming election, but he deftly sidestepped the subject. I also tried to sound him out on his wife's pet project, the proposed sexual reformation of England; but he wouldn't talk about that either.

Lady B-B, for her part, was equally taciturn. While she apparently had no qualms about discussing sex with me privately, she was the picture of rectitude in the presence of her hubby. I got the impression that sex was a word which never passed between them. Their idea of an exciting night in bed, I felt, would be a night when the B.B.C.'s equivalent of

Johnny Carson told a bathroom joke and they both giggled themselves to sleep.

As lunch dragged on—and believe me, it dragged—I found myself comparing Lady B-B's present comportment with her comportment when we had been alone together. Then she had been warm and outgoing; while she had mouthed all the antisex clichés in the book, she had nonetheless related to me on a healthy man-woman basis. Now, with Lord B-B around, she was inhibited as a mouse in a cat house. I tried to square away the image of the cowed wife with the image of the outspoken sexual reformer. I couldn't.

After lunch we adjourned to the patio for brandy. It came as something of a surprise to me that Lord B-B drank. Judging from what I'd seen of him so far, I'd expected that he didn't even belch, let alone indulge in one of the genuine vices.

A few minutes later I was in for surprise number two: he also smoked. As we sat looking out at the multi-acre expanse of rolling hills that constituted his back yard, he took a package of cigarette papers from one pocket, a pouch of tobacco from the other and deftly rolled his own.

We chatted for a while about such fascinating matters as the differences between the British and the American use of the article "an" and the relative merits and demerits of French versus Italian brands of mineral water. Then, as Lord B-B polished off his second brandy, I got surprise number three.

There was a birdhouse a few yards from the patio, and swallow was hovering over it. In front of the door was a horizontal perch, attached to the house by a nut-shaped joint which was situated in the perch's exact center. Lord B-B watched the swallow for a moment, then, nudging me with his elbow, said, "Which side of the perch do you think he'll alight on?"

"Huh?" I said, completely mystified.

"The swallow!" he said animatedly. "See him? He's getting ready to alight on the perch! Quick! Which side do you think he'll alight on—the left or the right!?"

"Beats me," I murmured, wondering what the hell he was getting so excited about.

"Dear," said Lady B-B, "I really don't think Doctor Damon is the gambling type."

He silenced her with a look. "Come on, Damon!" he told me. "Be a sport! Pick a side!"

"All right," I replied, "I think he'll land on the left."

"Five pounds says he lands on the right!" He whipped a wallet from his pocket, tugged out a five-pound note, and slapped it on the table in front of us.

I flipped a fiver from my roll onto the table. "You're on," I said, smiling inwardly because I suspected that I finally had found a chink in his armor.

The swallow hovered for a moment longer over the birdhouse, then slowly descended toward the center of the perch. Through the corner of my eye I watched Lord B-B. He was on the edge of his seat, using body english to steer the bird toward his side of the perch.

"Come on, baby!" he cried. "The right! The right!"

Sure enough, the swallow landed on the right side. Lord B-B triumphantly scooped up the two five-pound notes. "Told you he'd land on the right, Damon! Told you!"

"So you did, sir. So you did."

He looked at me evenly. "Damon, I get the impression that you're a man after my own heart—a gambling man."

"You're so right," I deadpanned. "I'm a gambler's gambler. You name the proposition and I'll bet on it." Actually I ordinarily wouldn't bet a nickel on a leadpipe cinch. But I had a mission to perform, and anything that got me closer to Lord B-B would make my work easier.

"Glad to hear that, Damon," he enthused. "I'm a gambler's gambler myself. No point in living if you aren't willing to take a few chances now and then, that's what I say." His eyes took on a fervent look. "The young set, they don't know what a pleasure it is to take your risks with Lady Luck. They're too wrapped up in sex and music and all that nonsense. But we mature fellows, we know what real excitement is. We know where it's really at." His eyes rolled heavenward. "Gambling, that's where!" he exclaimed, banging his fist on the table.

"Speaking of sex," I began, seizing the opportunity, "tell me—"

"Sex?" His brow furrowed. "Who was speaking of sex?"

"You were," I reminded him. "You said that young people are too wrapped up in sex and music . . ."

"Did I say that?" he cut me off. "I couldn't have. There are four subjects I absolutely refuse to discuss: sex, politics, religion and literature."

"Why not literature?" I asked, puzzled.

"Where's the gamble in that?" he snapped.

"Point taken. But, getting back to sex, Brice, you were talking about it. I'll lay you odds of eight to five you were talking about it. Lady Brice-Bennington is our witness."

"A wife can't testify against her husband," he said peremptorily. "And I never talk about sex, politics, religion or literature. So there's no bet." He poured himself another brandy. "But let's get back to our conversation about gambling, shall we? It's not often that I meet a fellow devotee. Everyone nowadays seems all wrapped up in sex and music and all that nonsense."

"Okay," I replied, letting the second mention of sex go by the boards unchallenged, "let's talk about gambling. Better yet, let's place another bet. I've got one I think you won't be able to resist."

He grinned. "Let's hear it!"

"Two M.P.'s I'm interested in are up for election in a few weeks—Christopher Smythe and James Whelan. What kind of odds will you give me on their chances of reelection? Make it a parlay bet if you like, or make it two individual bets."

His smile was that of a mother who catches her son with his hands in the cookie-jar. "Sorry, Damon. That's politics. And there are four subjects I absolutely refuse to discuss——"

"I know," I groaned wearily. "Sex, politics, religion and literature. But, Brice, old chap, I'm not asking you to *discuss* politics; I'm asking you to bet on an election."

"Sorry, Damon," he smiled patronizingly, "a man's got to stick by his principles, and mine are——"

"All right, already, don't make a federal case out of it."

"A federal case? What do you mean?"

"Never mind. It's just an American idiom."

"Ah yes, quaint idioms you people have over there. One wonders how the language ever got distorted so." He took out his tobacco pouch and package of cigarette papers and repeated the Bull Durham bit. "Do you smoke, Damon?" he asked, almost as an afterthought.

"Yes," I said, setting him up for what I was sure would be another long-lost-brother routine, "I smoke a great deal. Unfortunately, though, I don't care for the tobacco in commercially manufactured cigarettes. I prefer a stronger blend."

"Then you roll your own?" he asked excitedly.

"Yes. My tobacconist back in the States imports a special blend for me from Turkey. I brought a kilogram with me to London, but it was stolen from my hotel room the night I got here. I haven't had a cigarette since—and, frankly, I could use one."

"Then try my blend!" he exclaimed, almost falling out of his chair in his rush to hand me the mixings. "It's Turkish also! I think you'll love it!" Turning to his wife, who had remained silent throughout our conversation, he said, "By Jupiter, Penelope, I think I've found a truly kindred spirit here in Damon!"

I took a cigarette paper from the package, folded it and poured some tobacco inside. I wasn't an expert roller like Lord B-B, of course. But back when I started smoking, cigarette money was hard to come by, and most kids broke in on roll-your-owns. I hadn't entirely lost the knack.

He watched me, and evidently was satisfied that I wasn't too clumsy. "Here you go, Damon!" he smiled, lighting a match and holding its flame to the tip of my cigarette. "Take a healthy lungful and tell me what you think."

I inhaled deeply. The smoke felt like sandpaper as it went down my windpipe, and I had all I could do to keep from coughing. But I kept a straight face, held the smoke in for a few seconds, and managed a smile as I exhaled.

"Well," he prodded, "how do you like it?"

"Not bad!" I said enthusiastically. "Not bad at all!"

"By Gad, Penelope," he chortled, "I've found me a fellow connoisseur! Brilliant idea of yours, bringing Damon over here! Tell me, Damon, how'd you like to join me some evening at my club for a bit of poker?"

"My favorite game, Brice. My favorite game."

"Well, I say! That's really good news! Penelope, I think this is a cause for celebration. Bring out the amontillado."

Lady B-B promptly disappeared inside the mansion, returning a few minutes later with a bottle and two fresh glasses. Lord B-B filled one for each of us, and we toasted.

"To all suitors of Dame Chance, whatever the means by which they urge their suit!" he intoned.

"Bottoms up!" I replied, hoisting my glass.

By this time, my friend the Lord had polished off three brandies. These, combined with the amontillado, were putting him in a very mellow mood.

He suggested three more proposition bets—one involving an ant that was crawling across the patio floor, another involving the number of words on the amontillado label, another involving a second swallow who was about to alight on the perch which the first swallow had abandoned. The wager each time was five pounds, and I beat him two bets to one.

We drank some more amontillado, and he got mellower still. We exchanged a few racetrack and card-table anecdotes. Then he had second thoughts on my earlier suggestion that we bet on the Smythe-Whelan election.

"It occurs to me, Damon," he said, his speech slightly slurry, "that you were right when you said that betting on an election isn't the same as discussing politics. As a matter of fact, if we positively refuse to discuss anything about the election we're betting on, the bet should be most interesting."

"Most interesting indeed, Brice. Now, if you recall, I had suggested that we could place either a parlay bet or individual bets. What sort of odds will you give me each way?"

He smiled knowingly. "*You* give *me* the odds, Damon. It was you who suggested the bet."

"But," I argued, "you live here and I don't. You know more about the candidates' chances than I do."

"Perhaps. Then again, perhaps not. After all, you wouldn't have suggested betting on this particular election unless you had some idea of what the outcome would be."

"Point taken." I smiled magnanimously. "Therefore, I'll give you the odds. Would you prefer a parlay bet or individual bets?"

"Parlay, of course." His expression, and the speed with which he answered the question, testified to his belief that no true gambler would bet anything but the parlay.

Or maybe, I suddenly realized, he had another reason for betting the parlay. Maybe he had a very good reason to believe that whatever happened to Smythe would also happen to Whelan—because the scandal his wife planned to set off would ruin them both.

"Very well," I said. "Since I think both races will be runaways, I'll set odds of eight to five. Pick the two candidates you think will win. If they both do, you win my eight. If only one of them does, or if neither of them does, I win your five."

"Those are tough odds. I should think you'd be a bit more generous."

"Tough or not, they're the odds I'm setting. If you like, you can set the odds and I'll pick two candidates."

"No, no," he said quickly, "I'll play with your odds."

Smiling fraternally, he added, "You drive a hard bargain, but, of course, you wouldn't be a real gambler if you didn't."

"All right, eight to five. I'll cover all bets up to five hundred pounds."

He whistled under his breath. "Five hundred pounds! You *are* a real gambler!"

"Pick your candidates," I replied.

He pursed his lips thoughtfully. "Can't be too hasty about this," he muttered. He took another sip of sherry and rolled a fresh cigarette, offering me the mixing to do likewise. After I had, he lit both our cigarettes. Then, studying the smoke that was rising from his, he said, "I'll bet the full five hundred pounds. And the candidates I'm betting on are Davis and Hull."

Davis and Hull—Smythe's and Whelan's opponents! Both were pro-Communist. And Lord B-B was supposed to be anti-Communist. Of course, he didn't necessarily have to favor the candidates he was betting on. But the London newspapers seemed to think that Smythe and Whelan were a shoo-in. Perhaps Lord B-B knew something that the papers didn't—for example, that a scandal was about to break.

"You're on," I told him. "My eight hundred pounds are yours if Davis and Hull both win. If not, your five hundred pounds are mine."

"It's a deal," he said, sealing it with a handshake.

We drank some more amontillado and placed a few more proposition bets. Then, telling me what a pleasure it had been having lunch with me, he excused himself to attend to some business chores. I was left alone with Lady B-B.

"I suppose you're eager to get back to work, Doctor," she said, sounding very much as if she wished I weren't.

"Not really," I replied. "I'd just as soon spend a little more time with you." Smiling warmly, I added, "We have many things to discuss."

She smiled back and I noticed that she no longer seemed inhibited. Evidently she loosened up whenever her spouse wasn't around. "What things?" she asked.

"Well, for one, my survey. I've accomplished a lot this morning with Miss Stark and her assistants, and I imagine you'd like to be kept abreast of developments. And I'd also like to discuss your own sexual views in greater detail than we did yesterday."

Her smile broadened. "Fine, let's discuss both subjects

—but not right now. I have some business to attend to myself this afternoon, and it really can't wait."

"Then when can we have our discussion?"

"At tea—if you're free."

I grinned. "At tea it shall be, Lady B, at tea it shall be."

I spent the rest of the afternoon with Gretchen Stark and her crew. Old Gretch and the girls were so efficient that by teatime not only had the four random samples been selected but the questionnaires I had designed to be administered to them had also been stenciled, mimeographed and packaged for delivery. Since Gretchen and the girls were going to do the initial interviewing, I now had nothing more to do until the replies had been assembled and tabulated, which meant that I had about ten days to devote uninterruptedly to solving the mysteries of the Smythe-Whelan affair.

As things now stood, there were plenty of them, but thanks to my little chat that morning with Andi Gleason, I had a theory which answered all of my questions.

It went like this:

Andi Gleason and Diane Dionne were a pair of small-time hookers who had a friend—perhaps a pimp—with big ideas. Somewhere or other along the line, this friend had been given reason to believe that Smythe and Whelan could be induced to respond favorably to advances by Andi and Diane. He then arranged things so that the girls would meet the M.P.'s, and a pair of discreet and clandestine affairs began.

Somehow or other this friend of Andi and Diane had figured out a way to get Smythe and Whelan hooked on the girls—so hooked that they couldn't terminate the affair. He then began shaking down Smythe and Whelan for cash, but he had misguessed the amount of cash they would be good for. When he found that the money wasn't there, Andi had to go back to work at The Safari Club to help pay the bills while he figured out some other way to exploit the gold mine he believed himself to be sitting on.

Surely he must have realized that the newspapers would pay dearly for the girls' personal stories of their affairs with the M.P.'s. Christine Keeler, after all, had cleaned up better than a million dollars in royalties after the Profumo scandal broke, and Mandy Rice-Davies, who hadn't even been involved with Profumo, cleaned up another half million for her story.

But the friend of Andi and Diane evidently thought he could do even better than this (how, I couldn't yet guess), and so he had ordered the girls to keep seeing the M.P.'s until it was time for him to make his big move.

Now, somewhere along the line, the Communists must have gotten wind that the M.P.'s and the girls had something going, just as The Coxe Foundation had. They assigned some agents to the case, trying to get proof which would be sufficient to set off a scandal. If they actually got the proof they wanted, they probably were holding it over Smythe and Whelan's heads in an attempt to blackmail the two M.P.'s into revealing what they knew about the B-bomb. Or, if they didn't yet get the proof, they were still hunting for it—whether they knew about the B-bomb or not.

As concerned the Friends, they too had gotten wind that something was brewing with Smythe and Whelan and the girls. But, since they really weren't too good at playing the spy game, they never got the proof they needed to set off a scandal that would get Smythe and Whelan turned out of office. Now they had stopped looking, and were concentrating instead on other means of helping Smythe and Whelan's opponents. They evidently thought they had the situation well under control—witness Lord B-B's confident bet on the election—and so there was no immediate danger that the scandal would ever break.

As concerned who was tailing me, the answer was simple: the Communists. During the course of their routine tail on Andi, they had picked up on me. I had been involved in enough missions for The Coxe Foundation—some of which involved my working hand-in-hand with Russian agents—that I was recognized immediately as an American spy. I therefore was being tailed in the hope that I could lead the way to paydirt which the Commies hadn't been able to strike on their own.

That was the theory, and it touched all the bases. If it was correct, my mission would be a cinch. All I'd have to do was spirit Andi and Diane out of England and the ball game would be over.

Unfortunately, I had a sneaking suspicion that my theory wasn't correct. True, it answered all my questions. But it answered them too well.

Spy mysteries aren't supposed to be solved this easily. There's always supposed to be a fly in the ointment, a missing link that makes it impossible to string a chain of apparent coincidences together and come up with a rational explanation for everything that's been happening.

My theory was too pat.

It made no allowance for a missing link.

And while, when I was a novice at the spy game, I might've been all set to close the case at this point and compliment myself on a job well done, I now was more skeptical than proud. I had a feeling—a feeling so strong that it almost gave me goosebumps—that something would happen any second now that would dash my theory to hell and leave me even more mystified about the Smythe-Whelan affair than I had been when I started in on the case.

I mentally rehearsed every aspect of the case, but couldn't come up with the missing link I was looking for. So I ran the whole works through my mind one more time. I still couldn't come up with the missing link.

I was about to do another replay when Lady Brice-Bennington showed up for our appointment. She was wearing a bright pink dress with a neckline that was—for her, anyway—extremely daring, and the look in her eyes said that she couldn't wait for our planned sexual discussion to get underway. Next to Robbi Randall, perhaps, I would have found her downright unattractive. But Robbi Randall wasn't around, and Lady B-B was. I didn't have too many reasons to believe I'd score with her, and I had a lot of good reasons to believe that I wouldn't. But it sure as hell would be fun to try—and I planned to.

Damn the missing link, I told myself as I crossed the room to take her hand. Full speed ahead!

CHAPTER SEVEN

We had tea in the breakfast room at the Eros—but not before I had played another round of hide-and-seek with my tails. Note well: tails, plural.

Rumpled Suit led the parade. He was posted across the

street, pretending to read *The Evening Standard*, as Lady B-B and I pulled out of the mansion driveway in her sedan. Not giving any indication that he had seen us, he ducked into a phone booth and hurriedly dialed a number.

Next came a slim, dapper dude in an Edwardian jacket and mod, bell-bottom slacks. He was posted on the same side of the street as the mansion, and like Rumpled Suit, he was pretending to read a newspaper.

No sooner had he spotted us leaving the driveway than he made a beeline for a Volkswagen parked at the curb. As he got inside, I saw his face. I gulped. Tail number two was none other than Peter Blaine, the pimp.

I maneuvered Lady B-B's sedan around a corner and into the heavy traffic on Charing Cross Road. Blaine's Volks stayed right with us. Then, a minute later, an Austin-Healy slipped into line a few cars behind him. I couldn't be sure, but I was willing to bet that it was the same Austin-Healy that had followed Andi from my hotel that morning.

Just for the sport of it, I decided to give my tails a run for their money. Pulling off Charing Cross, I raced through a maze of side streets. Lady B-B's sedan was much too fast for the Volks. Peter Blaine dropped out of the running after I had turned the fourth intersection. I made a few more turns, then pulled to the curb and parked.

"Doctor Damon," said Lady B-B, bewildered, "what's the meaning of all this?"

"I suspect we're being followed," I said sinisterly.

"My word!" she gasped. "But in heaven's name, by whom?"

"A former girlfriend of mine," I ad-libbed. "She's madly in love with me, and she must've learned I'm in London. She wants me to marry her."

"Really, Damon, I must protest. I want no part of matters like these."

"Don't worry about it, Lady B. No one will ever know you're involved."

"But I'm not involved."

"Precisely. So there's nothing for anyone to know, is there?"

My verbal footwork was dazzling enough to silence her. We sat there for a minute or two waiting for the Volks. It never showed up.

But the Austin-Healy did. The driver had turned the last

corner too quickly to put on his brakes and stop casually somewhere behind me, so he just drove on by. I got a good look at him as the car passed. It was my monocled tablemate from the night before at The Safari Club.

I waited until the Austin-Healy was out of sight. Then I U-turned and doubled back to Charing Cross. Trying to make sure the Austin-Healy couldn't pick up on me again, I took the scenic route back to the Eros—via Buckingham Palace, then London Bridge, then Leicester Square—but he stayed with me until I had turned onto Shaftesbury Avenue, then, mysteriously, he lost interest and cut down Wimpy Mews.

I soon discovered why he had lost interest: he knew I was going back to the Eros, and he had me covered there. His colleague, Rumpled Suit, was sitting in the lobby reading *Punch* when I ushered Laby B-B in. He never gave any indication that he noticed me, but I knew that he had.

In the dining room, Lady B-B and I killed half an hour discussing my progress with the sex survey. Then I shifted the subject to her sexual philosophies and the experiences which had led to their development. We reworked most of the terrain we had covered the previous day, all without my discovering anything significant. Then our discussion became a debate; she presented the standard arguments against the free dissemination of erotic literature, and I presented the standard arguments for it.

My rhetoric, of course, didn't move her—not any more than her rhetoric moved me—but as we spoke I got the feeling that something else was moving her. In the course of arguing that the reading of erotic literature arouses people to perform sexual acts, she cited numerous passages from the erotic books she had read—in the course of her work, of course, and only, heh-heh, as a matter of duty. She described each of these passages in great detail, sometimes all but reciting them verbatim. And, with each passage she described, her manner grew more animated.

No doubt about it, she was excited. And her excitement wasn't the zeal of a missionary about to win a convert or a debater about to make a point. It was good, old-fashioned sexual excitement. She probably would be the last person in the world to admit it, but she was really getting turned on!

I suggested that we adjourn to my room to continue the discussion. She seemed to weigh the idea for a moment. Then she demurred.

"But why not?" I demanded. "Surely you don't think I'll attack you."

"Of course not," she replied quickly. Then, smiling seductively in spite of herself, she added, "But you might make sexual advances."

I smiled back. "I certainly would be tempted to. But, of course, I respect your wishes too much to surrender to the temptation."

"Suppose you got carried away?"

"I wouldn't." Leering, I added, "But, even if I did, you'd be able to resist them, wouldn't you? What was it you told me yesterday? 'The difference between humans and animals is that humans control their sexual impulses.' Surely you don't think you'd lose control."

Her pride in her control was her downfall. If she had admitted that she was afraid of getting carried away, I wouldn't have had a rhetorical leg to stand on. But she wouldn't admit it—probably not even to herself. And without admitting it, she couldn't logically decline my invitation.

Grinning like a bastard, I led the way to my room. She accepted my offer of a drink, and our debate resumed. Her argument this time was the old proposition that reading about sex gives people ideas that they wouldn't get otherwise. To support her position she offered the hypothetical example of a high school student who might happen upon a book describing precoital stimulation.

"Take a book," she said, "like *Sisters of Sin*—one of the many pieces of trash which presently circulate freely throughout England and which can be bought for a few shillings at newsstands near all our high schools. Have you read it?"

"No," I confessed, "I haven't."

Her eyes glowed with a missionary fervor. "Well, I have and I can tell you that it's absolutely disgusting. There's one scene, for example, where a lascivious old rake seduces a young girl. The description of the seduction goes something like this:

" 'Mister Dennison held Laurie to him, and his hand gently stroked the soft, firm mound of her breast through the fabric of her cashmere sweater. She wasn't wearing a brassiere, and her nipple came alive as he touched it. A shiver of excitement coarsed through her body, and, as if by reflex, her legs parted.

" 'Mister Dennison then brought his hand from her breasts to her thighs, which were bare, and he slowly worked

95

his way up their smooth surface until his fingers had come to rest against her panties, which were damp in anticipation. She wanted him desperately, and he knew it.' "

As had been the case in her previous recitations of erotic passages, Lady B-B seemed to grow more inflamed with each word she recited. Her eyes lost their missionary glow and took on a look that was pure hunger.

She continued, " 'Laurie's hips began moving slowly back and forth, as if in response to the prodding of a penis. Her thighs spread farther apart, and Mr. Dennison worked his fingers through the leg of her panties and began massaging her eagerly distended clitoris. She squirmed passionately in his lap. She knew that what she was doing was wrong, but she also knew that a lot of other girls did it, and she figured that it couldn't be wrong if so many people liked it so much.'

" ' "Laurie," Mr. Dennison said, "I would like to make love to you."

" ' "Oh no, Mr. Dennison," she replied, "we shouldn't. It's all wrong."

" ' "But Laurie," he argued persuasively, "a lot of other girls do it, and they like it very much. It can't be wrong if so many people like it."

" 'Laurie wasn't persuaded by his argument, but she now was too hungry for him to resist any longer. As his fingers left her clitoris and began to explore the moist warmth of her vagina, she said: "Okay, Mr. Denison, let's do it." '

" 'He then guided her panties over her hips, situated her on a couch and made love to her.' "

The Big Prig's eyes took on a sad expression.

"Continue," I prodded. "It's just getting good."

She frowned. "The passage ends there. The next passage takes up with Laurie in her eighth month of pregnancy at a home for unwed mothers."

"What a shame," I sympathized.

Her excitement now having ebbed, Lady B-B proceeded to point out the moral lesson which she believed the sexy passage proved. "Imagine, Doctor, a high school boy who has gotten his hands on this awful book. As he reads the passage, he first discovers that an effective way of getting a girl excited is to caress her breast. He then learns that one of the ways he can determine she is excited is by noting the tenseness of her nipple. He next learns that a further indication of excitement is the dampness of a girl's panties. And he then learns that he can get her all the more excited by massaging her clitoris."

"Not all females," I reminded her, "respond to the same modes of sexual foreplay, and not all have precisely the same bodily reactions to sexual arousal."

"That doesn't matter. The point is that a boy can learn some modes and some bodily reactions from one book and other modes and other reactions from other books, then put the knowledge together and use it against innocent girls. What's more, from these same books they can learn arguments by which to persuade girls to abandon their virtue. In *Sisters of Sin*, for example, Mr. Dennison tells Laurie that sex can't be wrong if so many people like it. How many boys, do you suppose, will repeat this argument in their own attempts at sexual conquest?"

"Frankly, Lady B, I don't think too many boys need Mr. Dennison's example. The thought that sex can't be so bad if it's really so good probably occurs to most people long before they've ever read an erotic book."

"Most, perhaps, but not all. And if even one person is prevented from learning the techniques of seduction, the Friends of Decency's campaign against erotic literature will have been a worthwhile endeavor."

I had half a dozen rebuttals just ready to be used, but I didn't use any of them. I was interested in turning The Big Prig on, not in playing Demosthenes, and my experiences thus far with her led me to believe that the best way to turn her on, and to keep her turned on, was to keep the conversation on a strictly sexual plane.

"Let's look at the matter from another angle," I said. "Let's forget about high school students for the moment and let's talk about married couples. Let's suppose that a husband who, thanks to your campaign to ban all erotic books, has never discovered that the clitoris is an erogenous zone. Let's suppose that this husband doesn't even know what a clitoris is, or that most women can't achieve orgasm without clitoral stimulation. Because of his ignorance, his wife goes sexually unsatisfied. And because she is unsatisfied, she commits adultery with a man who does satisfy her. Eventually she decides to leave her husband and live with her lover. She abandons him—and their children—because she couldn't find sexual satisfaction in their marriage."

"She doesn't *have* to abandon him. People can have a happy marriage without sexual satisfaction."

"They can? I don't think so."

"I do. And I'm in a better position to know than you are."

"How so?"

"I—I—" she fumbled. Then, catching herself on the threshold of what would have been a damaging admission, she said, "I've investigated dozens of such cases in my work for the Friends of Decency."

"Well," I replied, "I've investigated thousands of cases in my work for the League of Sexual Dynamics, and I've never found one couple that was perfectly happy without sexual satisfaction."

"You've evidently investigated the wrong cases, Doctor."

"I don't think so, Lady B. I think that you've been too biased in your investigations to admit that these couples of yours really weren't happy." Seeing an irresistible opportunity to get things back on a personal plane, I added quickly, "Take yourself and Lord Brice-Bennington, for example. Do you suppose that your marriage would be as happy as it is if he didn't satisfy you sexually?"

She blushed.

"Well," I prodded, "would it?"

Her blush deepened. "Doctor Damon," she said after a moment, "Lord Brice-Bennington and I are perfectly happy without sex."

I'd more or less expected the answer I got, and I was ready with a follow-up. "You mean," I asked, pretending incredulity, "that you don't engage in sex?"

"That's right."

"Have you ever?"

"Never."

"But for goodness' sake, Lady B, why not? Surely you can't think that sex is evil *inside* a marital relationship."

"Not evil, Doctor. Just unnecessary."

"Strictly speaking, nothing is necessary—not love, not affection, not compatibility, not even cohabitation. But while unnecessary, they're all desirable—and so, I think, is sex."

"Not desirable for Lord Bennington and me, Doctor."

I scratched my head, thoroughly puzzled.

"Perhaps," she said after a moment, "I'd better explain."

"Perhaps," I agreed, "you'd better."

She took a small sip from the drink I had mixed her. It had gone untouched previously. "Doctor," she began, "I told you earlier that I had lived something of a hectic life before I formed the Friends of Decency. I told you that I had been to bed with many men, and that I found all my affairs unsatisfying, and that I subsequently came to see the error of my ways—which was why I formed the Friends. But I didn't tell you how I came to see the error of my ways."

"True," I observed, "you didn't."

"During my years as a playgirl, I found that men were interested in me for only one thing: sex. I despised the feeling I got after they made love to me—the feeling that I had been exploited, used, taken advantage of. I hated the life I was leading, and I wanted desperately to extricate myself from it. But I had grown too accustomed to soft living. I didn't have the strength to make a clean break . . . until I met Lord Brice-Bennington."

"You met him while you still were a playgirl? I thought you hadn't met until after you had formed the Friends of Decency."

"No. It was largely because of his influence that I formed the Friends."

I suddenly gave myself a very swift mental kick in the pants. One of the reasons I'd been unable thus far to understand Lady B-B's warmth and friendliness to me was because I assumed she was flying the Friends' flag under her own colors. Now I saw otherwise—and I should have seen it all before.

When I had examined Walrus-moustache's dossiers, I had noted that Lord and Lady B-B were married a year after she had formed the Friends. I had automatically assumed that she must have met him during the course of her work as a bluenose and that he had fallen for her because he thought her to be a kindred spirit. What I had overlooked was that some people wait awhile before they get married—especially if they think of marriage as a sacred and indissolvable bond.

So Lord B-B met her while she was still a playgirl. And, judging from what she had said, he had sold her not only on abandoning the libertine life but also on organizing the anti-sex pressure group which she now headed.

That explained the difference in her attitude when she was in his presence and when she was alone with me. Unless I missed my guess, Lady B-B was only the figurehead of the Friends of Decency; Lord B-B was its brains, the man who directed its actions from behind the scenes, the *real* Big Prig.

The question now was: How had he managed to get Lady B-B under his control?

I had no sooner thought it than she proceeded to answer it.

"Lord Brice-Bennington and I," she said, "met through mutual acquaintances. One of my girlfriends was at the time dating Sir Cecil Applewaithe, who was a very good friend of Lord Brice-Bennington. Lord Brice-Bennington had a reputation among his friends as somewhat of a social recluse, a man who never went out with girls and who never seemed to have any inclination to. One night, I later was to learn, Sir Cecil had gotten Lord Brice-Bennington drunk and had questioned him about his sex life, which Lord Brice-Bennington most certainly would never have discussed while he was sober. Lord Brice-Bennington then admitted that he was a virgin."

"At age thirty-five?" I gulped.

"At age thirty-four, actually, but I suppose one year doesn't really make that much difference. In any case, Sir Cecil tried to persuade Lord Brice-Bennington to try making love with someone—a prostitute, perhaps, or a partygirl. But Lord Brice-Bennington wouldn't hear of it. He felt that sex was debilitating and that it dissipates one's mental energies, and he was for that reason determined to remain a virgin for the rest of his life. That, by the way, is why he now refuses to discuss sex with anyone; he finds it tedious to have to defend his views among people who invariably will not understand them anyway."

"You're digressing," I reminded her. "How did Sir Cecil finally bring you and Lord B-B together?"

"He capitalized on my husband's proclivities as a gambler. He told Lord Brice-Bennington that he believed him to be a hypocrite, and he bet the Lord a substantial amount of money that the Lord wouldn't be able to stick to his beliefs about sex if he happened to be in the company of a sexy young girl who was trying very hard to get him aroused. Lord Brice-Bennington accepted the wager, and Sir Cecil arranged through my girlfriend for me to be the girl who was supposed to arouse him. We went to the theater together, and afterwards out for a few drinks, and finally back to my flat, and the whole time I did everything in my power to awaken his sexual interest. But I failed miserably. Meanwhile he succeeded in awakening my interest in—and my appreciation of—the ascetic life.

"He pointed out to me that there are untold intellectual pleasures available to those of us who choose to use our brains, and that by shutting off our sensual activity we enlarge our capacity to experience intellectual pleasure. I had never heard a man talk like this before, and it fascinated me.

"Lord Brice-Bennington fascinated me too—I mean as a man. He was sophisticated, urbane and attractive. More im-

100

portant, he was interested in me as a person, not merely as a recipient of his sexual excesses. He was the only man I ever dated who didn't try to seduce me. And yet, though we had no sexual bond, he still was interested in me. We dated again and again. The more we saw of each other, the closer we became. I came to share his ascetic views, and I found with him greater satisfaction than I ever had experienced with any other man.

"After we had been seeing each other for a year, he suggested that we attempt to share our bliss with the countless millions of people who had been misled into believing that sexual pleasures were preferable to intellectual pleasures. He thought that this goal could best be accomplished if we were to form an organization which would stamp out all smut and filth in England. He reasoned—and I accepted his reasoning completely—that if people did not constantly find themselves surrounded by sexual stimulation they would turn to intellectual pursuits and learn of the joys to be had in intellectual activity. But he also knew that people would be less likely to accept an anti-smut organization if it was headed by a man rather than a woman. They would think of a male reformer as another Anthony Comstock—a person whose own sexual inadequacies had turned him sour on sex. Meanwhile, if a woman who had engaged in extensive sexual activity headed the organization, people would accept her as a genuine reformer, as a person who had walked the path of sin and finally saw the error of her ways. I was the perfect woman to head this organization, and I did. With Lord Brice-Bennington's never-obvious help, I formed the Friends of Decency.

"Within a year, thanks to the contributions of church groups and others who were opposed to filth and smut, the Friends had become a thriving organization. By this time, Lord Brice-Bennington and I had been married. Five years have passed since then, Doctor, and not once during those five years have we even kissed. Yet I've been completely happy, and so has he."

"How do you pass your time without sex?" I asked acidly. "Playing tiddlywinks?"

She smiled patiently. "Engaging in intellectual pursuits, Doctor."

"Like betting which end of the perch a swallow is going to land on?" My sarcasm was so thick you could cut it with a knife.

Her smile now wasn't merely patient; it was patronizing.

"His mania for gambling is one of his private pleasures, and one which I don't share. Our mutual pleasures are all intellectual."

"For example?"

"Conversation, mostly."

"I thought he didn't discuss sex, politics, religion or literature. What else is there to talk about?"

"He doesn't discuss these subjects publicly," she said, eyes ecstatically aglow. "But he discusses them with me—privately and intimately."

Well, no doubt about it, Lord B-B wasn't merely The Big Prig, he was also a first-class nut—and his wife apparently was as nutty as he was. But I wasn't interested in evaluating their sanity; I was interested in getting into Lady B-B's pants. And I suddenly thought of a way to do it.

"What I can't understand, Lady B," I told her, "is how you could give up a vigorous sex life like the one you led as a playgirl and not miss the pleasures of sex. I'm inclined to think you never really discovered genuine sexual pleasure."

"I discovered all there was to discover," she replied, a bit too defensively. "In three years, I had more than a hundred lovers."

I smiled sagely. "It's not how much meat one eats that counts, Lady B. It's the quality of the meat."

"I think my meat was pretty high quality."

"In other words, your lovers were physically attractive. But how skillful were they in satisfying your sexual appetites? How many of them brought you to orgasm?"

She blushed.

"Did any of them, Lady B?"

"Well, Doctor," she said quickly, "as *you* certainly should know, not all women have the capacity to experience orgasm. Kinsey pointed out that forty percent of all women never do."

"You're misinterpreting the statistics, Lady B. It's true that forty percent of Kinsey's respondents said that they never had experienced orgasm. But his survey was conducted in the early 1950s and dealt with sexual experiences before the sexual revolution. A far greater number of women today have been relieved of the sexual hang-ups that prevent orgasm, and the percentage of those who don't is considerably lower. Moreover, the fact that some women don't experience orgasm doesn't necessarily mean that they can't experience orgasm. Virtually everyone has the capacity—if properly stimulated."

"I don't agree with you. I think that there are some people

102

who can't experience it, no matter how they're stimulated."

The opening was perfect and I dived right in. "Let me prove my point by the most convincing proof available—experimental data."

"You mean—?" Her face reddened.

I grinned. "Precisely, Lady B. Let me demonstrate that I can bring you to orgasm."

"Why—why—why that's outrageous! How dare you even suggest such a thing?"

"My motives, madame, are not lustful. I'm merely trying to prove a point."

"B-but you're asking me to—to—"

"I'm asking you, Lady B, to act like the intellectual you claim to be. An intellectual never closes his mind to an argument he finds provocative. He investigates the argument and determines whether it has any real merit."

"But—but—"

She was weakening, and I knew it. It wasn't my logic that was swaying her. It was her bottled-up sexual desire—five years' worth. My logic was merely giving her an excuse to follow her natural inclinations—inclinations which had been apparent to me from our very first meeting.

"Investigate my argument, Lady B," I pressed. "Let me attempt to stimulate you with the sexual techniques I've learned during years of intense research. I've never yet met a woman I couldn't bring to orgasm."

"But—but what about my husband? What would he say?"

"That depends on the results of our experiment. If I fail to bring you to orgasm, you'll be able to tell him that you proved the great Doctor Damon wrong, that you proved that not all women can be brought to orgasm. Think what a feather that would be in your cap. Lord B could only applaud your victory against an enemy of the Friends of Decency. If, on the other hand, I do bring you to orgasm, you can employ on Lord B the same sort of logic I've employed on you to persuade him to experiment. He'll make love to you, and, after you've taught him all my techniques, he'll be an even more satisfying lover than I was because of the emotional and intellectual bond between you. What's more, he'll enjoy sex himself, and your marital pleasures will be both sexual and intellectual. Either way, you can't lose." I grinned. "And, of course, if you think that Lord B really would disapprove of this intellectual experiment, then you need never mention it to him. I certainly don't plan to tell him about it, and I'll be the only other person who'll know what has taken place between us." My grin vanished, and I stared intently into her eyes. "What's your decision, Lady B? Will you act like a true intellectual? Or will you retreat behind a wall of prejudice and fear? Will you be an owl or an ostrich?"

My reasoning, of course, was far from irrefutable. But then, Lady B-B was hardly the intellectual iceberg she liked to think of herself as. She had wanted me all along, and now she wanted me more than ever. I had given her an excuse to salve her conscience. She promptly took it.

"Doctor Damon," she said resolutely, "I'm going to be an owl. On with the experiment!"

The experiment began—slowly. I knew that my chances for success would be greatest if I got her to relax, so I worked like a devil at it. Lying next to her on the bed—with both of us fully clothed—I began kissing her gently on the lips. But I didn't touch any other part of her body, and I didn't induce her to touch any part of mine.

After a few minutes she said, "Really, Doctor, I don't see the point of all this. I've kissed men before. You're not going to bring me to orgasm this way."

"I'm conducting this experiment," I replied softly but firmly, "so we'll do things my way. That means, number one, you're going to stop addressing me as 'Doctor' and start addressing me by my first name, 'Rod.'"

"Okay . . . Rod," she agreed softly.

"Number two, stop trying to see the point of what I'm doing. Don't ask yourself if you're being aroused, or if a specific type of foreplay is going to bring yourself to orgasm. Just let what happens happen. If you like what I'm doing, go ahead and let yourself like it. If you don't, tell me that you don't like it and I'll do something else."

"Okay."

One thing she liked, I quickly realized, was being told what to do. She seemed to take genuine pleasure out of acquiescing to my demands. As I spoke to her, she grew more relaxed, and her breathing deepened in response to my kisses.

I proceeded from gentle kisses to those of a more passionate variety. My tongue entered her mouth. She received it hesitantly at first, then much less hesitantly. "I like that," she murmured appreciatively when I paused to come up for air. "I like that very much."

"So do I," I replied truthfully. "And I think we're both going to like the next part of the experiment even more. What

I want you to do now is think of a passage from one of the erotic books you've read, a passage about a man undressing a girl. Then I want you to describe it to me as accurately as you can. I'm going to keep kissing you while you describe it, and, at the same time, I'm going to do to you whatever the man does to the girl in the passage."

"What's the purpose of that?"

"Never mind the purpose," I snapped impatiently. "Just do it."

Actually, of course, there was a very definite purpose to it. Lady B, though she probably would be the last person in the world to admit it, was an erotolaliac—that is, a person who derives sexual pleasure from using sexual words and phrases, and from reciting sexual descriptions. I realized that earlier when I observed how excited she got as she quoted me the erotic books she was condemning. Now I planned to combine her erotolalic excitement with the excitement of tactile stimulation. The combination, I was sure, would really get her worked up.

It did. The passage she selected came from an uninspired hack-novel titled *Back-Seat Love*. It described the undressing of a reluctant teenager by the boy with whom she had been going steady since her freshman year in high school.

" 'As they sat in the back seat of his car which was parked in a darkened corner of a neighborhood drive-in theater,' " Lady B-B began reciting, " 'David slowly began to unbutton Judy's blouse.' "

On cue, I went to work on Lady B-B's buttons. At the same time, I held my mouth near hers and touched her lips and face provocatively with my tongue.

" 'Judy had mixed feelings,' " Lady B-B continued, breathing a bit more rapidly. " 'She liked to have David touch her, but she was afraid that it would get her too excited. She had never gone all the way with him, but she had come close. She didn't know how close she could come without losing her will to resist.

" 'David clumsily palmed one of her breasts. His heart was beating frantically, and he struggled to'—mmmmmmm, Rod, I really like the way you're kissing me now—'he struggled to get his hand underneath her brassiere, which fit her very tightly.' "

Not letting up on my kissing, I paralleled David's progress. I was sure that I wasn't as clumsy as he was when I palmed Lady B's right breast. But I had one hell of a time getting my

105

hand under her bra. It was so tight I wondered how she was able to breathe.

" 'Judy wanted David to touch her bare breasts,' " Lady B went on. " 'She had let him do this often in the past, and she liked the way his hands felt against her smooth, soft skin and her tender, little-girl's nipples. She turned toward him, so that he could unhook the straps of her brassiere and touch her breasts more easily.' "

Good girl, Judy! I thought to myself. For a minute there, I had been afraid that Lady B's Iron Maiden bra was going to break my fingers.

Following Judy's lead, Lady B turned toward me. I promptly unhooked her bra—a C-cup, judging from the fact that there were three hooks on the strap—and covered her bare breast with my hand.

It was a surprisingly large breast—full, firm and exquisitely shaped. The nipple leaped to life as my palm moved over it, and Lady B squirmed delightedly in response to my touch.

" 'David unhooked Judy's bra, then brought his hand back around to the front of her body and covered her bare breast with it,' " Lady B continued, the narrative lagging behind my progress. " 'His fingers tickled her nipple, which hardened as he touched it. He took it between his thumb and his forefinger and began rolling it gently back and forth, which excited her all the more and made her nipple grow harder still.

" 'Mmmmmmmmm," moaned Judy, very excited by what was happening to her.

" ' "Do you like what I'm doing to you?" David asked.

" ' "Oh yes, David," replied Judy. "Oh yes. It feels so wonderful."

" ' "David then switched to the other breast, taking the nipple of this breast between thumb and forefinger, just as he had taken the nipple of the previous breast. The second nipple quickly became just as hard as the first nipple had, and Judy's body came alive with an exquisitely exciting sensation.

" ' "Do you like this, Judy?" David whispered softly.

" ' "Oh yes, David," she replied in hoarse tones. "Oh yes, I like it very much."

" ' "David then reached under Judy's loosely hanging brassiere with both hands and began tickling both nipples at once.

" ' "Do you like what I'm doing to you now, Judy?" he inquired, panting heavily.

106

" ' "Oh yes, David," she answered, panting also. "Oh yes, I like it even better than the other way.' "

I wished to hell that David and Judy would knock off the chit-chat and get down to some more serious business. But Lady B-B evidently thought their rate of progress was just fine. As I copied David's actions, she grew more and more excited, and punctuated her narrative with an increasing number of *mmmmmmmm*'s.

David continued to fondle Judy's breasts for what must have been five or six pages—all of which Lady B recited without omitting a single "Oh yes, David." The appreciative adolescent's nipples were palmed, fingered, stroked, squeezed, pinched, rubbed, rolled and tweaked. Also, her breasts proper were kneaded, gyrated in clockwise and counterclockwise circles, pressed against each other, pulled away from each other, pressed against her chest, pushed up as far as they would go, stretched down as far as they would go, and maneuvered in every other conceivable pattern of angles and arcs. No doubt about it, David—or the author of *Back-Seat Love*—was a dyed-in-the-wool breast man.

Finally the hand action gave way to mouth action. Now David went through a whole symphony of oral foreplay techniques. Judy's nipples were nibbled on, licked, lapped, tongued, sucked on vigorously, sucked on gently, raked over by David's teeth, and flickered over and round by his fast-moving tongue. Then, her apparently tireless lover went to work on her breasts proper, licking, lapping, sucking, nibbling, gnawing, biting, chewing, et cetera. About the only thing he didn't do was shove her breasts in his ears, and, as Lady B-B's narrative—and my dutiful duplication of his deeds—continued, I wondered if he wouldn't eventually get around to even that.

He didn't. Fortunately, after what had to have been at least a dozen pages of *Back-Seat Love* the oral phase ended and the genital phase began.

" 'David,' " Lady B recited, " 'reached under Judy's skirt and maneuvered her panties down her thighs and removed her panties.

" 'Judy was reluctant to let him do so. She had gone this far with him only once before, and she had become so excited that it took all the will power she could summon to refrain from going all the way.

" 'However, she was too excited now to offer anything but
107

token resistance. David quickly overcame this resistance, and her panties soon lay on the floor of the back seat of the car.

" 'Stroking her thighs provocatively, David worked his way up to her vagina, which was damp with anticipation. He maneuvered his fingers between the twin folds of skin which lay at the organ's opening, and after caressing her there for a while, he slowly eased his middle finger up inside her.

" ' "Oh, David," Judy gasped.

" ' "What's the matter, Judy?" he replied. "Don't you like it?"

" ' "Oh yes, David," said she, "I like it very much. It feels wonderful. But, David, I'm scared."

" ' "What are you scared of, Judy?" he asked.

" 'She whispered the words fearfully: "I might get pregnant and have a baby."

" 'He smiled reassuringly, all the while continuing to massage her vagina excitingly with his middle finger. "Judy," he said, "a girl doesn't get pregnant just by having a boy touch her."

" ' "I know, David," she replied, "but I'm getting very excited by having you touch me"—as indeed she was—"and I'm afraid that if you don't stop soon I won't be able to resist when you want to go all the way."

" ' "I won't want to go all the way, Judy," he promised her. "Just trust me."

" ' "I trust *you*, David," she answered. "It's myself that I don't trust."

" ' "Don't worry about trusting yourself, Judy," said he, massaging her vagina even more vigorously. "I promise you that I won't put you in the situation where you'll have to trust yourself."

" 'She did not know whether to believe him, but by this time she was too excited to offer further resistance. "Okay, David," she said naively, "you may continue to touch my vagina. But please, David, please, please, please don't get me too excited."

" ' "I won't, Judy," he grunted, knowing full well that this end was precisely what he had in mind. "I promise you I won't."

" 'He then proceeded to insert a second finger inside her vagina, and to maneuver both fingers back and forth in semicircular motions. As might have been expected, these motions were sufficient to arouse her to a point where her

108

resistance vanished completely, and there, on the back seat of his car, they had sexual intercourse.' "

"What?" I gulped, brought up short by the abrupt ending. "The passage stops there?"

"Yes," replied Lady B. "That's the end of the chapter. The next chapter begins with Judy in a sleazy abortionist's office in Liverpool."

I had a sneaking suspicion that Lady B was lying to me. I suspected that she herself had become so aroused by this time that she didn't want to delay the master stroke any longer, and that she consequently had done a very quick editing job on David's genital foreplay.

"Take a passage from another book," I told her. "Make it one where a man and woman fondle each other genitally for quite a while."

"Really, Rod, that won't be necessary," she smiled, reaching, as if by instinct, for my manhood. "I'm quite ready for the climax of our experiment now."

Frankly, so was I. Progressing right along with David, and, in fact, going him one better, I had completely undressed both Lady B and myself. The presence of her succulently ripe, unbelievably neglected body next to mine, to say nothing of all that foreplay, had put me very much in the mood for the grand finale.

But I wasn't toing to take any chances at having the experiment end without her experiencing The Big Climax. "I'm conducting the experiment," I said authoritatively. "We'll do things my way, and my way means reading another passage."

Reluctantly she agreed to recite an excerpt from *Lust Weekend*, a novel about a Mersey housewife's affair with a plumber from Nottingham. The plumber was an intravaginal genius *par excellence* who had an especially keen talent for clitoral massage.

Midway through the passage, Lady B went wild. She was involved in a description of the plumber vigorously but gently rubbing his finger back and forth across the housewife's clit when suddenly she stopped reciting and cried, "Oh, Rod! Oh, my heavens! What's happening to me?"

I covered her mouth with mine and thrust my tongue deeply inside. At the same time, I began rubbing her clit even more rapidly and with my free hand I cupped one of her marvelous breasts and began kneading it vigorously.

"Mmmmmglrubbbb!" she groaned, struggling against me.

Her heels dug into the bed, and her hips arched high into the air. Her body was taut as a violin string.

I rubbed her clit all the more rapidly. Her hips began pumping back and forth in a furious pantomime of coitus. She struggled even harder to free her mouth from mine. Finally she succeeded.

"Rod!" she screamed. "Oh, Rod! Take me! Oh! Oh my God, I can't believe it! It's happening! Rod!"

The tremors that shook her were like fierce waves in a frantic sea. Her body arched so high in response to them that only her heels and shoulders were touching the bed. Then the tension snapped and she back to the bed only to arch up again as though she had landed on a trampoline. Her teeth bit hungrily at my lips, and the fingers of both her hands squeezed my staff as tightly as if it were The Staff of Life.

"Ohhhhhhhhhh!!!" She wailed. "Oh God! Oh Rod! Oh, it's still happening! It isn't stopping! It—it—ohhhhhhhhhhhh!!!"

Working like a bastard, I stoked her to even higher peaks of passion. There were five years of dammed up sexual energy inside her, and the dam had now burst. I drew every last ounce of ecstasy out of her, and then, as her sensations ebbed and she coasted down gently from her pinnacle of passion, I held her to me and kissed her lovingly on the lips.

"Ohhhhhh," she moaned softly, her body fluttering like a leaf in my arms. "Rod, I can't believe it. I never dreamed that there was a feeling like this. And I never thought it would happen to me. But it happened. It really happened."

I smiled as I eased open her thighs. "Penelope, dearest, it's going to happen again."

It did—again and again and again.

Having gotten her machinery into good working order, I proceeded to work it at full capacity.

For openers—and for my own satisfaction as well as hers—I gave her a course in love-making doggie-style. This permitted me to massage her all-important clit at the same time that my manhood was rutting around inside her. Her vagina was, at first, as tight as a new pair of shoes. But the muscles loosened up as our act continued, and I was able to do all my tricks without hurting her.

Meanwhile, I discovered that she had a few tricks of her own. As our bodies grew accustomed to each other, the techniques which she had employed in her mattress days as a playgirl all seemed to come back to her. She had a super-talented muscle that seemed to have a will of its own. It gripped me and released me, squeezed me and stroked me.

And her hips were something else. They wriggled and writhed, bounced and jounced, dipped and dived, swung and swung some more. All sorts of crazy sensations came alive inside me, and I responded with a performance that far surpassed my usual superb level of excellence. My actions in turn prompted reactions, and her reactions prompted further actions on my part. Together we were one fantastic, superbly coordinated, incredibly efficient sex machine—a machine with billions of complex moving parts, all working harmoniously toward the same end: mutual satisfaction.

And mutual satisfaction it was. I forced myself to hold back as long as possible so that she could get as good a ride as I could possibly give her, and she had a good half-dozen orgasms to my one. But my one was worth all the effort I had put into it, and then some. Like wow!

When we finally severed the tie that binds, she was a devout and dedicated convert to sexuality's cause. But I still wasn't ready to rest on my laurels. Enticing her to recite another passage from the erotic books which she previously had claimed to despise, I set up a little game of Sixty-Nine. Then we went at it again in what the Polynesians call "the missionary position," meaning man-on-top, woman-on-bottom, an arrangement which Christian missionaries to the South Seas had endeavored—unsuccessfully, to be sure—to persuade the islanders was the only ethical permissible mode of coital congress. Next I gave her a shot of what Benvenuto Cellini once described as *amore all'Italiana*, or "love, Italian style"—translation, buggery. And, for a finale, we went a round standing up, her back to the wall so that my thrusts had an even more telling effect on her.

When we finally called it quits, the time was nine o'clock and Lady B-B was barely able to walk. "I say, Damon," she grinned ecstatically, "you argue a good case. I came here believing I was incapable of orgasm, and I'm leaving having experienced all of twenty of them."

"Such, Penelope," I replied suavely, "is the power of the scientific method. When in doubt, investigate. Empirical data are vastly superior to hastily formed prejudices. Et cetera, et cetera, et cetera."

Her eyes took on a dreamy look. "I can't wait to share my data with Lord Brice-Bennington." Then, her expression sud-

111

denly clouding, she said, "But how will I go about it? I can't just waltz up to him and announce that you've taught me what sex was all about."

"For the time being," I said, "don't tell him anything. I've got an idea about how Lord B-B can be brought into the fold. It'll take me a few days to set things up, but once I have, everything'll work out just dandy. Meanwhile, act as if nothing had happened between us, and I'll let you know when we're ready to make our big move."

"Whatever you say, Rod," she purred, buttoning her blouse. Then, kissing me resoundingly on the lips, she bade me goodbye.

She hadn't been gone for five minutes when my phone rang. The caller was the desk clerk, who informed me that a messenger was on the way with a package for me. The package proved to be the bundle of newsclips about Smythe and Whelan which I had asked Walrus-moustache to have The Coxe Foundation's London crew assemble for me.

I put it in the drawer of my bureau, then took a quick shower and dressed for dinner. Then, giving myself a once-over in the mirror before leaving for the restaurant, I flashed an ecstatic smile.

"Damon, you old dog," I said aloud, "you've done it again—and in record time."

I was really proud of myself. In a few hours, Andi Gleason was due to come calling. When she did, I was sure, I'd have no trouble persuading her to head for that little rose-covered cottage in San Francisco—and to take Diane Dionne along with her. Meanwhile, while I waited for her to arrive, I'd go through the newsclips I had just received and uncover a clue which would magically explain just why the guy who had put Andi and Diane up to extorting Smythe and Whelan believed that the two M.P.'s were such lucrative targets. When I had found the clue, I'd be able to prove to Walrus-moustache that the attempted shakedown of Smythe and Whelan hadn't been a Communist plot at all, but merely the brainstorm of a small-time pimp, Peter Blaine, whose plans far outdistanced his ability to execute them. I'd thus be able to prove that the Communists never knew that Smythe and Whelan were involved with the B-bomb—in fact, that the Communists never knew that the B-bomb existed—and that they had been tailing Andi and Diane only because they were trying to get some proof of the rumors about Smythe and Whelan, rumors which would die once Andi and Diane were safely spirited away to the States. I'd also be able to prove that the Friends of Decency had been fishing around with Andi and Diane for the same reason that the Communists had—to get proof of the scandalous rumors—and that the proof had not been forthcoming. And, as a bonus, once I'd done my little number on Lord B-B, the Friends of Decency would be dissolved, and The Big Prig, along with his Big Prigess, would be two of the most devout converts to *la vita sessuale* since David discovered Bathsheba.

"Missing link!" I scoffed, looking lovingly at my image in the mirror. "What missing link!? Your theory was correct all along, Damon-you-old-dog. You were just being paranoid when you doubted yourself. This case has just been wrapped up and tied in a neat pink ribbon. It's all over now but the shouting."

Adjusting my tie, I strode out of the room as proud as a Congressional Medal of Honor winner on Memorial Day. In the lobby, I tossed a contemptuous glance at Rumpled Suit, who was at his usual post, and paused long enough to buy an evening paper just to make sure he didn't fail to notice me. Then, tucking the paper under my arm, I ambled across the street to a Greek restaurant, where I gorged myself on shish-kabob and ouzo until I thought it'd come out of my ears.

"Damon, Damon, Damon," I told myself as I floated back up to the room. "You're a genius. An absolute genius. A man among men. A king among kings."

And boy did I regret saying it a few hours later!

"Pride," someone once observed, "goeth before the fall."

Well, I'd had my moment of pride—and I'd savored it.

Now for the fall. I only hoped I would survive it.

CHAPTER EIGHT

In my room, I tossed my unread evening paper on the dresser and opened the package of newsclips which The Coxe Foundation had sent me. It took better than an hour to find the clips I was looking for, but when I found them, I was more convinced than ever that my theory about the Smythe-Whelan affair was one hundred percent foolproof.

The first significant clip was a year old. It was from the financial section of *The Times*, and it stated that one Christopher Smythe of Kensington had inherited all the stock in a South African diamond mine. The value of the mine had been set at better than ten million pounds, or twenty-four million American dollars.

The second significant clip was also from *The Times*, but this time from the news rather than the financial section. It was six months old, and it stated that M.P.'s Christopher Smythe and James Whelan had been requested by the Prime Minister to divest themselves of their holdings in a certain American publishing firm which specialized in erotic books. The American firm, it seemed, had worked out a deal with a British firm, which planned to issue English editions of all the American firm's books. Since Smythe and Whelan were two of Parliament's most outspoken proponents of a law which would abolish Her Majesty's Censorship Office, the fact that they held stock in the American firm was deemed by the Prime Minister to be a conflict of interests.

The third clip, this one from *The Daily Telegram*, was five months old and revealed that Smythe and Whelan had refused to sell their publishing stocks. The Prime Minister had then threatened to make an issue of the conflict of interests charge. But evidently he never carried out his threat, because there were no further clips which mentioned the matter.

The fourth clip—this from *The Sunday Mirror*—was six years old. It consisted of a photograph and a caption. The

114

photograph pictured a group of people at a theater opening. The people were identified in the caption as Christopher Smythe, his wife, James Whelan, his wife, Doctor Stephen Ward and an unidentified friend. Doctor Ward, of course, was the osteopath-socialite-playboy-pimp who had introduced Christine Keeler to John Profumo. His unidentified companion in the photo bore a striking resemblance to Christine's bosom buddy, Mandy Rice-Davies.

Having examined all four clips, along with the financial statements on Smythe and Whelan which The Coxe Foundation had sent me, I didn't have much trouble deducing the modus operandi of Peter Blaine, the presumed mastermind of the Smythe-Whelan caper. I also was able to make a very plausible guess as to why the caper had gone wrong.

Blaine evidently had been on the scene in London at the time of the Profumo scandal. He, Andi Gleason and Diane Dionne had not been members of the social circle in which Stephen Ward and his girls had moved. But Blaine had, along with everyone else who read the newspapers, seen the Ward girls make a bundle of money on the scandal.

Like most small-time pimps, Blaine had wished he had had a piece of the Ward girls' action. But, unlike most small-time pimps, who just wished and never did anything to make their wishes come true, Blaine had gone to work immediately on a plan to set up his own Ward-style association with British VIPs who could be lured into a Profumo-like situation.

In search of prospective suckers, he had checked out newspaper files for the names of VIPs who had been associated in some way or other with Ward in the days before the Profumo scandal broke. He had realized that few if any of these VIPs would get involved in a potentially scandalous liaison while the public's memory of the Profumo scandal was fresh. But he also had realized that libertines, like leopards who don't change their spots, don't abandon their libertine ways, and he had guessed—quite rightly, as later developments would prove—that some VIP's would be good targets a few years after the Profumo business had died down.

When he came upon the photo of Smythe and Whelan and their wives with Ward and the girl who resembled Mandy Rice-Davies—a photo published in 1962, a year before the Profumo scandal had broken—he had added Smythe and Whelan to his list of prospective suckers. He probably had made some attempts to get to other VIPs and had failed. In any case, he eventually had gotten to Smythe and Whelan, most likely rather recently, perhaps not sooner than a year and a half ago.

His initial plan of action, it would seem, had been to get just enough proof of scandalous doings that he could sell his girls' stories about their affairs with Smythe and Whelan to the newspapers. But then he had come upon the item in *The Times* identifying one Christopher Smythe of Kensington as the inheritor of a diamond mine fortune. Now, instead of shooting at the half million dollars or so which he might expect to gain by peddling his girls' stories to the newspapers, he had decided to shoot at a much more lucrative target—a piece of the twenty-four million.

He had made a blackmail pitch to Smythe; he had threatened that unless Smythe began paying him off very heavily, he would set off another Profumo-like scandal. Smythe had refused to pay; probably he had claimed that he was not the same Christopher Smythe who had inherited the diamond mine fortune.

As a matter of fact, he wasn't the same Christopher Smythe. The financial statement with which The Coxe Foundation had supplied me listed Smythe's net worth at approximately a quarter of a million dollars. But Blaine, of course, hadn't had access to a financial statement; consequently, he remained convinced that Smythe was a multimillionaire, and he had refrained from setting off the scandal while he searched for new ways of getting Smythe to come across with the money.

A short time later, Blaine had learned that Smythe and Whelan were connected financially via their mutual ownership of American publishing stocks. He now had had even more reason than before to hold back from setting off a scandal, and he had begun putting pressure on Whelan for money. But Whelan hadn't been able to pay him off either, because Whelan's net worth, according to The Coxe Foundation's financial statement, was even less than Smythe's. What Blaine hadn't known—and what I did—was that Smythe and Whelan's holdings in the publishing company amounted to less than a thousand dollars each.

Any way you looked at it, Blaine was in a bind. He couldn't set off a scandal without blowing all chances at the multi-million dollar payoff on which he had set his hopes. And yet, he couldn't get Smythe and Whelan to come across with the money—because, although he didn't know it, the money simply wasn't there.

Meanwhile, Smythe and Whelan's hanky-panky with Andi and Diane had begun to attract attention—attention on the part of the Communists, attention on the part of the Friends of Decency, and attention on the part of The Coxe Foundation. Blaine probably didn't know exactly who was tailing his girls or why; but he couldn't have failed to recognize that the girls were being tailed, and in an effort to take the heat off while he continued to search for new ways of forcing Smythe and Whelan to pay off, he had pulled Andi and Diane out of circulation.

That was when he found himself in an even worse bind. With Andi and Diane no longer able to earn money as hookers, Blaine's personal income was cut drastically. Eventually his fortunes had sunk so low that he was forced to put Andi back to work—not as a hooker, where she'd be an easy target for the people who were tailing her, but rather as a performer at The Safari Club. He had told her, of course, not to turn any tricks, and he had kept a close eye on her to make sure that she wouldn't.

She had, however, turned one trick—with me. And that, it now seemed, was going to spell curtains for Blaine. When she took me up on my offer to get her and Diane out of the country, Blaine would find himself without any girls whose stories he could sell.

Amendment: not *when* she took me up on my offer, but *if*.

She hadn't yet, and with every minute that passed, the "if" became bigger.

By the time I had finished with the data on Smythe and Whelan which The Coxe Foundation had sent me, the time was one fifteen. Andi had been due to visit me at twelve thirty. Punctuality was hardly her strong suit, but if she was really going to take me up on my offer, she'd hardly want to waste any time getting to me.

I waited. For fifteen minutes I paced the floor hoping against hope that the next minute would bring a knock on the door. Then I poured myself a Johnnie Walker Black and killed another half-hour sitting drinking it while I looked out the window. Still no Andi.

Another half-hour passed. I was as fidgety as a cat in heat. To take my mind off my problems, I tried working the crossword puzzle in my still-unread evening paper. Fifteen minutes and only two crosswords later, I gave up on the puzzle and tried reading the paper.

That's when, as the saying goes, the proverbial mustard hit the fan.

Good old Superspy Damon!

I'd talked myself into believing that there was no missing link in my foolproof theory.

I'd congratulated myself on wrapping up the case and tying the package with a neat pink ribbon.

I'd hailed myself as a genius, as a man among men, as a king among kings.

And I'd been so intoxicated by my heady brew of self-congratulation that I'd failed to notice the headline that screamed out from the front page of the paper in attention-demanding seventy-two-point type.

"SMYTHE," the headline read, "COMMITS SUICIDE."

The Smythe in question wasn't the gent from Kensington who had inherited the diamond mine fortune. It was none other than *my* Christopher Smythe, the M.P. He had cashed in his chips at four in the afternoon by firing a forty-five-caliber bullet into his head at point-blank range in the library of his home, to which he had retreated an hour earlier after telling his wife that he planned to work for most of the evening on a speech he was due to deliver in the House of Commons the following day.

Two columns away from the Smythe story was another story—this one headlined in thirty-six-point type and accompanied by a photograph. I noticed it only after I had read to the "continuation" line on the Smythe story and was about to turn the page. When I did notice it, I couldn't believe that I had carried the paper around with me for nearly four hours without noticing it before.

The headline read: "PLAYGIRL KILLED IN AUTO MISHAP."

The photo was a head-shot of Andi Gleason.

She had been killed, the story said, by a hit-and-run driver whose car had struck her while she was crossing the street in front of her apartment at five forty-five.

It took me all of half an hour to believe that Andi was dead. And it took an hour more to get over my shock. Somewhere or other during the time I'd spent with her the previous morning, I'd taken a liking to her. And while a no-nonsense professional spy might not let his feelings get in the way of his work, I—an amateur spy who hated the business

118

more and more with each mission—felt a very real personal loss and a sense of guilt. I was sure that the only reason Andi had been killed was because I had entered her life.

I finally pulled myself together, and after a few dry runs during which I read every word in her obituary without one word registering in my brain, I reread the obit with comprehension and analyzed it. My analysis led me absolutely nowhere.

Andi had been run down in the street. The police had no idea as to who ran her down, and they suspected that her death was accidental. The story identified her as a sometime prostitute and a stripper who was a favorite among the highly placed London gents who patronized The Safari Club. And that, except for a description of her injuries and a few biographical items that I already knew about, was all there was to it.

Now I had to figure out who had killed her and why—and what connection there might have been between her death and Smythe's.

My first fleeting thought was that Smythe might have run her down, then shot himself—that he, realizing that she had gotten him into a jam that he couldn't possibly get out of, killed her in a moment of passion, then killed himself because he knew that he'd eventually be identified as her murderer.

An interesting theory, but completely contrary to fact. Smythe, according to the newspaper, had shot himself at four o'clock—almost two hours before she was killed. One theory down; how many more to go?

I considered the possibility that Smythe had hired someone to kill her, then had suffered remorse and killed himself. But this was pretty far-fetched too. Smythe wasn't a gangster; he was a Member of Parliament. The modus operandi just didn't fit.

So, if Smythe hadn't killed her, who had?

Certainly not the Communists. Alive, she was potentially worth a great deal to them. Dead she was worthless.

Peter Blaine? Even less likely. With her dead, he had just lost his big chance to get at the twenty-four million dollars he believed Smythe possessed.

Was it possible that Blaine had killed her after Smythe's suicide—perhaps in a fit of anger, because he felt that she had failed to do her job with Smythe?

Possible maybe, but far from probable. Even with Smythe dead, Blaine might have sold Andi's story to the newspapers.

In fact, Smythe's suicide would make the story a lot more valuable than it had been while he was still alive.

So Blaine hadn't killed her either.

The Coxe Foundation, maybe?

Was it possible that Walrus-moustache, perhaps after learning through his own sources that the scandal was about to break, had ordered her killed because this was the only way to keep a lid on things?

No. Plausible though the idea was, I refused to accept it. Walrus-moustache had said that he drew the line at murder—and I believed him.

So back to the question: Who had killed Andi?

I'd just exhausted my list of candidates and didn't know where to turn next.

Before I had read the newspaper, I'd thought I had my case all wrapped up. My theory had touched all the bases, and there'd been no missing links.

Now there were missing links all over the place. There were so many damned missing links that I didn't even have a theory anymore.

The logical next move would be to hunt up Diane Dionne and try to spirit her out of the country. But even if I succeeded, there'd be no way of insuring that Blaine, and/or whoever else might have proof of a relationship between Andi and Smythe, couldn't set off a scandal.

Meanwhile, it was damned unlikely that I'd succeed. I had a list of places where Diane had been known to frequent. But after what had happened to Andi, Diane probably wouldn't want to touch me with a ten-foot pole, especially if Blaine had told her, as he almost certainly had, that Andi had spent her last night on earth with me.

Or *had* he told her? Perhaps not. The theory that made him the mastermind of the Smythe-Whelan caper had just been missing-linked to hell. The new mastermind could have been anyone from my old pals, the Communists, to my new pals, the Friends of Decency—or even some third party I'd never dreamed of. For all I knew, Blaine might have been following me when I left Lady B-B's mansion only because the doorman at The Safari Club had told him that I'd been looking for him!

What I needed now was a new theory. But I didn't know where to start constructing one. Several facts were indisputable:

(1) Christopher Smythe and James Whelan had been in a position to know something about Country X's B-bomb.

(2) Christopher Smythe and James Whelan had been carrying on affairs with Andi Gleason and Diane Dionne.

(3) Andi Gleason and Diane Dionne appeared to have been trying to shake down Smythe and Whelan for cash.

(4) The Friends of Decency appeared to have briefly investigated the possible connection between Smythe and Whelan and the two playgirls, then to have moved out of the picture.

(5) The Communists appeared to have investigated the possible connection between Smythe and Whelan and the two playgirls, and now appeared to be still very much a part of the picture.

Those were the facts.

Now to string them together and come up with a plausible explanation of everything that had happened, and why.

But I couldn't.

There were just too many damned things that had happened, and no theory could take all of them into account.

If the Friends of Decency had been behind the Smythe-Whelan caper, why hadn't they set off the scandal which could have been their only possible motive in setting up the affair?

If the Communists had been behind the caper, why had Andi Gleason been killed?

If Philip Blaine or someone like him had been behind the caper, why had Andi been killed?

Was it possible that Andi's death actually had been accidental, as the police believed? I doubted it. A girl who's deeply involved in intrigue of this sort doesn't just amble out into the street and get herself run down by a car. That's asking too much of coincidence.

Yet, if Andi's death hadn't been accidental, who had killed her and why?

And why had Christopher Smythe committed suicide?

I was right back where I started from—a lot of facts, a lot of suspects, and no way to string them all together.

What I needed was more information.

There's an old saying to the effect that if you can't get what you want you'd damned well better make do with what you've got.

At this point I had only two leads—Diane Dionne and Peter Blaine. Neither one of them seemed very promising. But they were all I had, and my only move was to play them for whatever they were worth.

121

Stuffing all the material The Coxe Foundation had sent me into my suitcase and locking it, I left the room. Rumpled Suit wasn't waiting for me in the Eros lobby, but he was waiting across the street, sitting behind the wheel of the familiar Austin-Healy. I trotted off in the direction opposite the one the car was facing, ran down a side street, and hailed a cab for Trafalgar Square. If the Austin-Healy had attempted to follow me, it hadn't made its U-turn soon enough, because neither it nor Rumpled Suit was anywhere in sight when I got out of my cab. Satisfied that I had shaken my tail, I hailed another cab—this one for my true destination, 14 Williamson Mews, London W1, the address on Peter Blaine's business card which the doorman at The Safari Club had given me the night before.

The building was a rundown brownstone that contained eight apartments. I pressed Blaine's buzzer, but got no reply. After buzzing him for a minute or two more, I pressed all the other buzzers. Finally I got an answering buzz, pushed the door open and went inside.

Blaine's apartment was on the top floor. I walked up the creaky stairs and rapped on his door. No answer.

The door had a single lock, the type which, as all second-story men know, can easily be picked with a credit card or some similar plastic or cellophane device. I had taken out my American Express card and had fitted it into the crack above the latch when a burly guy in a sleeveless undershirt materialized in the hallway behind me.

"What's your act, Jack?" he scowled.

I quickly sized him up. He wasn't carrying a weapon, and while he could easily have disposed of me with his bare hands, he didn't appear to be getting ready to make a move toward me.

"I'm Peter Blaine's friend," I said, forcing a feeble smile. "Do you know where he is?"

He planted his hands on his hips. "You're his friend, are you? Then why're you trying to pick his lock?"

"He said I could stay over in his apartment tonight," I ad-libbed glibly. "But he wasn't here when I got here, and I got tired of waiting out in the street."

Sleeveless Undershirt seemed uncertain whether to buy the explanation. "Look, Jack," he said after a moment, "I don't like the idea of having somebody ring my doorbell and wake me out of a sound sleep at two in the morning. Now, I don't care who's friend you are, you better get the hell out of here or I'm going to call the cops."

His request, all things being considered, was reasonable enough. In fact, I was damned lucky to get away without a broken nose. Smiling profusely, I apologized for having wakened him, then backed down the stairs.

On the main floor, I opened the door leading to the street, then closed it, but I stayed inside the building. Sleeveless Undershirt evidently had been waiting in the hallway for me to leave, because after I had closed the door I heard his footsteps retreat back into his apartment and the apartment door slam shut.

I gave him fifteen minutes to fall back asleep. Then, taking off my shoes, I tiptoed back up the stairs and had another go at Blaine's door. A few flicks of my American Express card later, it slipped open and I was inside the apartment.

The joint was a real rathole. It consisted of a living room, a bedroom, a kitchen and a bath, each messier than the other. Unwashed socks and underwear littered all the floors, and there were dishes thick with bits of decaying food in the kitchen. The furniture looked like it had come from a junkyard. And there was dust all over the place so thick you could write your initials in it.

I went through all the drawers and closets. Blaine, I promptly discovered, was a collector of dirty pictures. There were literally hundreds of photos of nude girls—some in conventional poses, others in more exotic poses with whips, chains, leather clothes, etc. And still others engaging in sex acts with men.

In one closet I found a stack of negatives and some photo developing equipment, along with a few reams of mimeographed circulars and several boxes of correspondence. Among his other activities, Blaine evidently ran a mail-order pornography business.

I carefully examined all the men in the photos. None resembled Christopher Smythe, James Whelan or anyone else whose face I recognized. But in a strongbox with a broken lock that I found in another closet, there was a batch of newsclips about Smythe and Whelan. Among them were all four of the clips which I had singled out from the shipment The Coxe Foundation had sent me.

"Ah, soooooo!" I whistled under my breath, à la Charlie Chan. Maybe my theory hadn't been so far off base after all!

Suddenly the wheels in my brain whirred into action, and I had a new theory. Actually, it was just the old theory in new clothes, and with a few new twists. But the new twists explained away most of the old unexplainables.

There were still a few holes in the theory, still a few missing links of the sort which I had come to expect all spy theories should have. But I had the feeling that I was on the right track, and that if I just kept going in the same direction I'd get to the bottom of the Smythe-Whelan affair damned soon.

Another look at the strongbox lock convinced me that I was on the right track. The lock was broken all right. But it had been broken—more precisely, jimmied—only recently. Amidst the old scuffs and rust marks which covered its surface were some brand-spankin'-new silver scratches, especially around the latch.

My brain was now spinning a mile a minute. I knew how the Commies had entered the picture and approximately when. I also knew that they didn't have any inkling about Smythe and Whelan's connection with the B-bomb. Within the past forty-eight hours they had come to suspect that there was something very big at stake in the Smythe-Whelan affair, something much bigger than they had ever dreamed. But they still didn't know just what. And if I moved fast enough, they wouldn't find out.

I also knew why Christopher Smythe had committed suicide. Weak though he had been in some respects, he had been damned strong in others. And he had been damned loyal to the anti-Communist cause, so loyal that he blew his brains out rather than let the Commies have a chance at picking them for info about the B-bomb.

I still didn't know who had killed Andi Gleason, or why. And I still hadn't come up with a satisfactory explanation for the earlier involvement of the Friends of Decency, or for Lord Brice-Bennington's confidence that Smythe and Whelan would lose the upcoming election. But I had a hunch that I'd be able to answer these questions soon—damned soon. Now if only I could find Peter Blaine and Diane Dionne!

I packed all Blaine's pornographic photos and negatives into a cardboard box, along with the Smythe-Whelan clips and everything else that had been in the strongbox. Then, giving the apartment a last once-over to make sure I hadn't missed anything, I taxied back to the Eros. I had the desk clerk store my cardboard box in the hotel safe, and gave him a twenty-pound tip to make sure that nobody else found out about it.

Then I phoned the number of Peter Blaine's business card and told his answering service to give the following message: "Blaine, I'm the only man in London who can save your skin. Contact me immediately at the Hotel Eros. Rod Damon."

I was pretty sure that Blaine would contact me as soon as he received the message. Unfortunately I couldn't be sure he'd receive it. If my new theory was correct, and I now was positive that it was, Blaine was presently holed up somewhere frightened out of his wits—so frightened that he'd never think of checking with his answering service.

Confucius say: If mountain won't come to man, man must go to mountain—or words to that effect. I couldn't be sure that Blaine would look me up, so I'd have to try looking him up.

The first place I tried was The Safari Club. It took me a while to get there because while I'd been phoning Blaine's answering service my old pal, Rumpled Suit, picked up on me again. This time another tail was working with him, a chunky Neanderthal type with a crew cut, and I had to play the taxi switch game four times, as well as do some fancy footwork through the Picadilly Circus subway station, before I could shake both of them.

Blaine wasn't at the Safari, but, of course, my money-hungry pal, the doorman, was. In exchange for a tenner he revealed that he hadn't seen Blaine since the night before. He also revealed that he hadn't seen Diane Dionne for better than a week. However, when I promised a hundred-pound reward for whoever sent Blaine or Diane to me first, he said that he'd try like a bastard to get in touch with them. I believed that he would.

From the Safari I went on to a discotheque called Chantilly Lace, which had been number one on the list of places where The Coxe Foundation had told me to look for Diane. Not surprisingly, she wasn't around. But a few bartenders and waitresses, inspired by fivers from my unlimited expense account, said that they knew both her and Blaine.

Everybody told the same story: Diane used to visit the disco often, but had stopped coming about a week ago and hadn't been seen since; Blaine was a less frequent visitor, and hadn't been seen in the past two weeks. Nobody knew where either of them could be reached, but when I announced my hundred-pound reward, everyone agreed to keep an eye out for them.

Over the next three hours I covered two more discos, a coffeehouse and two all-night restaurants. The story was the same in each place: Blaine and Diane were well-known but hadn't been around recently, and nobody knew where they could be found. By this time it was nearly seven a.m. All told I'd gone through more than a hundred pounds and had left my calling card with a couple dozen people. One thing was certain: If Blaine or Diane ever returned to their old haunts, they'd find out damned quick that I was looking for them.

There still were a few more places on The Coxe Foundation list where I might have looked, but they'd all closed, and even if they hadn't been I was too damned tired to do any more looking. Resolving to check them out the following night, I taxied back to the Eros. My second tail, Crew Cut, was at Rumpled Suit's usual post in the lobby, and he looked as tired as I was.

"Get a good night's sleep, you poor bastard," I said silently. "I'm going to."

CHAPTER NINE

The next two days passed uneventfully.

There were no follow-up stories in the newspapers on Andi Gleason's death, and there was nothing in the follow-up stories on Smythe's suicide that indicated the newspapers had any idea of his involvement with Andi.

I checked out the other places on The Coxe Foundation's list of Diane Dionne's old haunts, but without getting any closer to finding her. I also phoned Blaine's number regularly, only to be told by his answering service that he hadn't been in touch.

On the two occasions when I visited Lady Brice-Bennington's mansion, I found her very eager for me to set up the little deal I had told her about back at my hotel room—the deal I had planned to convert Lord B-B to the pro-sex team. But, until I got things straightened out with Blaine and Diane I didn't really want to get involved in anything I couldn't walk out on at a minute's notice.

I did get involved briefly in a little more love-making with Lady B-B. We knocked off a pair of quickies one afternoon in the Friends of Decency erotic library—a cute touch, I thought—and another quickie the next afternoon in the bathroom on the mansion's third floor (in the shower, as a matter of fact, which really turned her on).

I also almost had a shot at Robbi Randall. Almost, but not quite. I had called her aside to tell her of my progress with Lady B-B and of the deal I had cooked up to convert Lord B-B, a deal in which Robbi was to play a crucial part. She readily consented to play the part I had in mind for her. But she wouldn't buy my suggestion that she rehearse the part with me in advance. For a moment I thought I'd be able to persuade her. Then she evidently decided to do her method-thing right to the very end and I couldn't change her mind.

I might have sold her if I worked a little harder at it. But I didn't really feel like working. My mind was so occupied with the business of getting to Blaine and Diane that sex, even sex with a knockout dish like Robbi Randall, wasn't all that important to me.

Somewhere in London, M.P. James Whelan was walking around with information about Country X's B-bomb —information that would be invaluable to the Communists. I was rather sure that after Christopher Smythe's suicide they wouldn't try to high-pressure it out of Whelan—at least not for a while.

But with every day that passed, they were bound to grow more impatient. And even if they did resist the impulse to give Whelan the same high-pressure treatment which I was sure they had given Smythe before he blew his brains out, they'd be strongly tempted to use the evidence they had of a Smythe-Andi-Whelan-Diane liaison to set off a scandal that might possibly topple Prime Minister Wilson's government.

As long as I stayed on the scene, they'd be inclined to hold back. But the closer election day drew, the less inclined they'd be, because they really didn't know why I was there; they only knew, or suspected, that my presence was an indication that something big was brewing, something bigger than the scandal they could now set off.

Would they forget about the Something Big and settle for second best?

If I didn't make contact with Blaine and Diane, and damned soon, they very well might.

By the end of the second day, I hadn't come any closer to

making contact. I'd made a second visit to each of the places on The Coxe Foundation's list, and I'd visited the doorman of The Safari Club no fewer than four times. But none of the people on my payroll had heard anything about Blaine and Diane—or, if they had heard, they weren't telling me, even though I had now raised my reward to five hundred pounds.

I capped off my second day with a round of drinks at The Rusty Flange, one of the discos on The Coxe Foundation's list. Then I headed back to the Eros. As usual, my Commie tails—by this time there were three, an arty mod type having joined Crew Cut and Rumpled Suit—were in the lobby. I ignored them, ambled up to my room and went to bed. My last thought before I dropped off to sleep was a prayer-like plea to the Law of Averages. "Law, old buddy," I murmured, "if you're ever going to throw me another bone, do it now."

Believe it or not, the prayer was answered. My phone rang at nine the next morning, and my friendly desk clerk informed me that there was a man waiting to see me in the lobby. The man, so the clerk informed me, said that it was a matter of life or death that he see me immediately, and offered as an inducement the cryptic message that "Peter had sent him."

Peter. Since I usually don't think too clearly before noon, it took me a minute to realize just who Peter was.

Then the message came through and I leaped out of bed as fast as greased lightning, scampered into my clothes and tore down the stairs. The messenger, a scrawny kid in his early twenties who looked like a refugee from The Rolling Stones or one of the other British pop music groups, was waiting for me at the desk. I gingerly steered him past Mod Type, who was standing outside the hotel pretending to read *The Morning Telegram,* and into a luncheonette a few doors away.

Blaine's message was direct and to the point: He was scared witless and wanted me to accompany the messenger to an apartment a few blocks from the Eros, where both of us could put our heads together and work out a deal.

My reply was equally direct and to the point. "Let's go!" I told the kid.

Mod Type picked up on us as we left the luncheonette. I hustled the kid through the Piccadilly Circus traffic and down into the Underground—as the British like to call their subway. Mod Type stayed with us, boarding the same coach that we did and standing a discreet twenty feet away.

I waited until the second stop, then, clutching the kid by

128

the arm, propelled him out onto the train platform. Mod Type, using the coach's other door, followed suit.

Still clutching the kid, I turned a sharp right and started down the platform, as if I was heading for the escalator leading to the street. Mod Type followed us closely.

But I didn't head for the escalator. When the kid and I reached the dor of the next coach, I slipped inside, pulling him behind me. Mod Type made a lunge for the door closest to him, but didn't reach it in time. The door closed in his face, leaving him standing on the platform.

At the next stop, the kid and I got off the train and rode the elevator to the street. Then I hailed a cab for the address where the kid told me I'd find Blaine.

The building was a sleazy, three-story walk-up that looked like a decent wind would knock it over. The apartment the kid led me to was on the third floor, and looked even rattier than Blaine's own apartment. Blaine was there all right—and so was Diane Dionne. He looked like he hadn't bathed or shaved in three days and smelled it too. She looked even worse than he did, although, thanks to the camouflaging effects of perfume, her odor wasn't quite so bad.

Blaine, who had been hunched over a kitchen table drinking a cup of tea, got up to greet me. Diane, who'd been lying on a nearby couch clad only in a see-through nightie, stayed where she was. The faraway look in her eyes told me that she'd had some tea also—only not the kind you drink in a cup.

"I hear you've been looking for me, Damon," Blaine said. "What can I do for you?"

"I'll tell you in a minute," I replied. "First let me tell you what I can do for you."

"Heyyyyy," murmured Diane, off on her own private cloud, "you're groovy. You talk like Paul Newman."

Ignoring her, I gave Blaine my planned pitch. I told him what I knew about his scheme to exploit Smythe and Whelan's libertine appetites. I spelled out the shakedown angle, which he had developed after learning that a certain Christopher Smythe of Kensington had inherited a twenty-seven-million-dollar diamond fortune—a certain Christopher Smythe whom Blaine had mistakenly assumed to be M.P. Christopher Smythe. I also spelled out my hunch about how the Communists had muscled in on his caper. Only I didn't tell him it was a hunch; I pretended that Andi Gleason had told me about it that night she came to my hotel room. His unprotesting look assured me that my hunch was right on target.

"Blaine," I concluded, "I'm the only guy who can bail you out. You've got evidence on Smythe and Whelan that can set off a scandal that'd blow England sky high. The Communists don't want that scandal, because they're playing for bigger stakes. And they'll do anything to keep you from lousing up their scheme—even kill you. I don't want a scandal either. But I'm with a nicer group than the Commies. If you play ball with me, I'll get you and Diane out of England safely. You can spend a year or so in the States at my government's expense. Then, when things cool down here, you can come back."

"A rose-covered cottage in San Francisco," Diane purred dreamily. "Andi told me about it. I always wanted to live in San Francisco." She smiled ecstatically and raised herself slowly to a sitting position.

Blaine paid no attention to her. To me, he said, "How do I know I can trust you?"

I shrugged. "You don't. You've got to gamble. Either you take your chances with me, or you take your chances with the Communists. It's your choice."

He thought about it silently. Diane, meanwhile, got up from the couch and staggered toward the bathroom door. "The Communists," she began, "killed——"

But she didn't complete the sentence because instead of going through the door she walked smack into the doorframe and fell to the floor.

I helped her to her feet. She wasn't hurt—just discombobulated. "Thanks," she told me, rubbing her forehead where it had hit the doorframe. Then, as if her initial train of thought hadn't been interrupted, she said, "The Communists killed Andi."

The Communists, I knew, didn't kill Andi. Suddenly, thanks to Diane, I had an explanation of Andi's death, an explanation that I kicked myself for not having come upon earlier. And with the explanation I'd pieced together the last important missing link in the Smythe-Whelan puzzle.

There was one more missing link—Lord Brice-Bennington's confidence that Smythe and Whelan would lose the election, coupled with the Friends of Decency's earlier prowling in search of proof that could be used to set off a scandal. But this missing link didn't really matter anymore, because I now had the puzzle solved.

Yep, it was all solved—neatly boxed and tied up with a little pink ribbon. Now all I had to do was deliver the package to The Coxe Foundation.

"Well, Blaine," I prodded, "how about it? The Communists killed Andi. Who's next. Diane? You?"

"They won't kill me," he said. "They won't kill me until they get the negatives."

"The negatives of the pictures you took of Smythe and Whelan? They don't need them. You had prints of the negatives in your apartment, and the Commies got them a couple nights ago when they burglarized your apartment. That's why Christopher Smythe killed himself. The Commies approached him with the prints and demanded some top-security information—information that's very important to them. Smythe knew they had him over a barrel, so he took the only way out. He shot himself."

"I have other negatives."

"What other negatives?"

"Negatives of the Communists. When they caught on to my thing with Smythe and Whelan and the girls, they tried to pump the girls for information. They hired the girls as prostitutes and tried to get them drunk, so they'd talk. While they were in bed with the girls, I took pictures of them."

I gulped. This was an unexpected bonus—a very unexpected and very desirable bonus but I didn't let Blaine know how excited I was at my discovery.

"The negatives are useless to you," I said. "What can you do with them? Mail them to the Kremlin?"

He sighed. "You're right, I guess. I showed some prints to Michaelson, the guy that's running their show. I told him I'd give him the negatives of him and his guys with my girls if he backed out of my caper with Smythe and Whelan. He laughed in my face. I figured he was just bluffing, but maybe he wasn't."

"You know damned well he wasn't. Even if he was worried about what you could do with your photos of him and his guys, he'd have nothing to worry about once you and Diane were dead. That's why you and Diane are hiding out here—and that's why you wanted to talk to me."

He left the table, walked to the window, and stood looking out at the street, his shoulders hunched forward in a posture of total defeat. "You win, Damon," he said softly, not looking at me. "I had a nice thing going for me, but it got out of control. I want out."

131

"I'll get you out. All you've got to do is play ball with me."

"Like how?"

"First off, give me everything you've got on Smythe, Whelan and the Communists. All the negatives, all the prints, and whatever other evidence you have."

"Okay. The whole works is in a safe deposit box at my bank."

"Do you have the key with you?"

He turned from the window, took the key out of his pocket and held it up in the air. "Will you put Diane and me on the plane for the States if I give it to you?"

"Not immediately. Once I check the box and find out you haven't been holding out on me I'll put Diane on a plane. You'll have to hang around London for a couple more days and do a few more favors for me."

"What kind of favors?"

"Number one, I want you to set up an orgy. I want five of the sharpest chicks you can get your hands on—real knockouts, and all dynamite in bed. Get them lined up and have them ready for me. I'll tell you exactly when I want them and where I want them to go. Can you handle it?"

"Yeah, but what's this all about? You're not going to keep me here just so I can get you laid, are you?"

"Never mind why I'm keeping you here. Just do what I tell you. Now, favor number two: I want some of the best grass you can get your hands on—kief or hashish if you can manage it; if not, marijuana'll do."

"Jeez, what the hell is this? You playing games with me, or what?"

"Never mind. Just get the grass. Can you?"

"How much of it?"

"An ounce."

"Only an ounce? For Chrissakes, I can give you that now —top grade hash, straight from Morocco."

"I'll take it."

"Okay, what else?"

"Just one thing more. I want you to show up at the orgy. And before you show up I want you to make the rounds at The Safari Club and all your other old haunts, and let everybody see you."

"That's suicide. If Michaelson and his guys see me, I'm a dead man."

"You'll have three bodyguards—three United States agents

132

who'll make mincemeat of Michaelson and his boys if they even try to get near you."

"But why, Damon? For Chrissakes, why?"

I grinned. "I'll tell you all about it some day in San Francisco, Blaine. Meanwhile, just do what I say." Winking, I added, "It's either that or take your chances alone with the Commies."

He looked at me for a moment as if trying to make up his mind. Then he tossed me the key to the safe deposit box. "You want the hash now or later?" he asked. "Now," I said. While he was getting it, I added, "Line the girls up for me on the phone, if you can, or send your friend here for them. I don't want you to leave this apartment until my bodyguards come for you. They'll get here in twelve to twenty-four hours at the latest. Meanwhile, keep Diane here while I check out the safe deposit box. If everything's all right I'll be back for her in about an hour, and I'll have her on a plane an hour or so after that. One more thing: Don't let her have even a sniff of grass or anything else. I want her as sober as she can be for the trip."

He gave me a small pouch of hashish, which I tucked into my jacket pocket. Hesitantly he shook my hand. "I hope you're playing straight with me, Damon," he said softly. "If you aren't . . ."

"I am," I smiled. "You can count on it." Then I gave Diane a goodbye peck on the cheek and scooted out the door.

"He's groovy," I heard her say as I exited. "He talks just like Paul Newman."

Out on the street, I hailed a cab for the American Express office. There I placed a long-distance call to my contact number with The Coxe Foundation back in the States. I couldn't get to Walrus-moustache personally, but I was sure my message would reach him soon enough.

The message was straight and to the point: "Andi Gleason dead. Diane Dionne will be on a plane to the States this afternoon. All ready to wrap things up, but need a little help. Have a dozen of the best men you can find report to my hotel room at the Eros as soon as possible. They should be heavily armed."

From American Express I went to Blaine's bank. Sure enough, his safe deposit box contained the negatives of Smythe and Whelan frolicking with Andi and Diane. But those negatives weren't nearly as interesting as the others in the box

133

—all of which were clipped to four-by-five prints, which made it very easy for me to recognize the people involved.

One of the people was Rumpled Suit. He was sixty-nining with Diane.

Another was Crew Cut. He was going at it doggie-style with Andi.

Another was Mod Type. He was doing the missionary position with Diane.

Another was my one-time tablemate with the monocle. He was doing a double-shot with Andi and Diane. On the back of this print Blaine had written: "Michaelson." How about that!? He was the leader of the gang!

There were a few more photos of guys I didn't recognize. Evidently the Commies had half their London crew working on the case. From the looks of it, they were really enjoying their work.

But then, who wouldn't? It sure as hell beat searching through newspaper files and tailing leads, which was the way the average spy spends most of his time.

I put the negatives and prints back into the safe deposit box, locked it, pocketed the key, and hustled back to my hotel room. Mod Type was on duty outside the hotel, and Rumpled Suit was in the lobby. No question about it; the pressure was really on.

In my room, I unlocked my suitcase and took out a doctored American passport. It contained a photo of Diane, along with a bogus American name and identification. Walrus-moustache had included it among the dossiers so that I'd be able to hustle Diane out of England on a moment's notice without any difficulty at the customs office.

Tucking the passport inside my jacket pocket, I left the Eros. Mod Type and Rumpled Suit picked up on me naturally enough, but the noontime pedestrian traffic in Piccadilly Circus was frantic and I managed to lose myself in the crowd. Just to make sure that they weren't still with me, I did a few turns through the underground and a few double-taxi dodges. Then I headed back to the apartment where Blaine and Diane were holed up.

Diane still hadn't come down from her high, but she was in a lot better shape than she had been when I left. I rode out to Heathrow Airport with her and got her on a flight for Dulles International Airport in Washington. After phoning the flight number and projected time of arrival to The Coxe Foundation contact number in the States, so that a Coxeman would be sure to meet her, I took another cab to the Brice-Bennington mansion. Lord and Lady B-B were just sitting down to tea when I arrived, and they promptly invited me to join them. Needless to say, I just as pro .ptly accepted the invitation.

"Pity that old Smythe did himself in, isn't it?" observed Lord B-B, sipping his tea.

"I didn't realize you were fond of him," I replied.

"I wasn't, old man. As a matter of fact, I thought he was quite a cad. But, don't you see, he's ruined our wager. One obviously can't win an el_ction if one is deceased, can one?"

"No," I admitted, "one obviously cannot."

"Unless," he put in quickly, "you'd be willing, Damon, to let the bet stand with whichever candidate his party picks to run in his place . . ."

"Sorry, Brice," I said, smiling, "the bet's off."

"I'd consent to a reduction of the odds. Say six to five?"

"Sorry, Brice."

"Then perhaps some other contest? There's a devilish lot of candidates seeking one office or another, you know."

"Sorry, Brice, No bet."

"I thought so," he said, scowling. As an afterthought he added, "Damned unstable people, committing suicide and whatnot."

I chuckled. "But cheer up, old man. I've got a wager in mind I think you'll find interesting."

His eyes widened. "Really!"

"Yes. A wager at odds I think you won't be able to resist. Say five to one on each of four contests. Or if you like you can improve the odds by parlaying a bet."

He all but jumped out of his seat. "Do say! What sort of contests?"

"Well, let me put it this way: You've bet on horse races, haven't you? What I have in mind is something like that, but infinitely more difficult to predict the outcome of."

"Well, stop shilly-shallying and tell me about it!"

"All right. I'm talking about a sex race."

He stiffened. "Did I hear you correctly, Damon? Did you say 'sex race'?"

"My exact words, Brice. My exact words."

"Damon, I told you before, there are four subjects I positively refuse to discuss: sex, religion, politics and——"

"Literature. I know. But I'm not asking you to discuss anything, Brice. I'm just asking you to bet, just like I asked you to bet on the Smythe-Whelan election. What I have in mind is this: A few friends of mine are planning an orgy, and I just figured that you and I might——"

"An orgy!" He as aghast. "Damon, how dare you suggest——"

"Odds of five to one, Brice. On each of four contests. And you can improve the odds by choosing to parlay one bet. All we've got to do is go to this orgy and——"

"Damon!" He was white as a sheet. "Lady Brice-Bennington is present!"

"Don't worry about me, dear," Lady B-B put in quickly. "If it amuses you, I don't object to your going to the orgy with Damon."

"Penelope," he replied tartly, "I think you'd better leave the room"—pause—"lest I offend your sensibilities when I tell Damon in the strongest possible language what I think of his indecent proposal."

"Whatever you say, dear," she smiled, exiting gracefully.

When she was gone, he turned to me with clenched jaws. "Damon, I don't take kindly to your unspeakable crudity. Penelope is my wife, and—"

"Brice," I interrupted, "I'll cover all bets up to a thousand pounds. That's four contests at a thousand pounds each. With odds of five to one, if you win all four contests, you can win twenty thousand pounds—that's forty-eight thousand American dollars. All on an investment of four thousand pounds."

"Unthinkable!" he whispered. "Imagine! Betting on sex! I've never heard of anything so indecent in my life!" But something in his voice told me he was weakening.

"Or you can improve your winnings by choosing to parlay on one bet of a hundred pounds," I reminded him. "You pick the order of finish—one through four. Your winnings if you get number one right will ride on number two and so on. If you win all four, you'll win—let's see—one times five is five, five times five is twenty-five, twenty-five times five is one twenty-five, and one twenty-five times five is six twenty-five—sixty-two thousand five hundred pounds. Brice, that's a hundred and fifty thousand dollars, and all on an investment of only one hundred pounds."

"You couldn't cover that," he snorted.

"My League for Sexual Dynamics could. And I am my league."

"No!" he said firmly. But he was sitting on the edge of his
136

seat. "I wouldn't dream of betting on sex! Why, I've never imagined—" He suddenly leaned toward me. Speaking in a whisper, he said, "Understand, Damon, I'm not going to participate in this proposed wager, but tell me, just out of curiosity, do you people in America bet on these things as a matter of course?"

"All the time," I grinned

"Do say! And precisely what does the contest involve? Not that I'd dream of betting, you understand, but, after all, I am a gambling man—as, evidently, you are—and I must confess that I'm a bit curious. What precisely do you bet on?"

My grin broadened. "Well, there are five men and five women. The men are in one room and the women are in another. The bettors are in the same room as the women, and the women are nude to give the bettors an opportunity to assess their sexual properties. Now, the person who is placing a bet estimates which of the women, based on his assessment of her sexual attractiveness, will bring her partner to orgasm first, which will bring her partner to orgasm second, and so on. When the bets have been made, the men come in and choose their women at random and on a signal they begin copulating with them. The man who has an orgasm first naturally stops copulating, as does the man who has orgasm second, et cetera. Every one called right in individual betting pays off. In parlaying it you win only if you call the first four right."

"Indeed! Why, that's fascinating! Not, you understand, that I'd consider betting on such a contest. But I'll admit, Damon, it *is* one deuce of a wager. Why, if a chap guessed four right on a parlay, he'd win a small fortune. And the investment would be almost negligible."

"Negligible indeed, Brice, but, as you say, you wouldn't consider betting on such a contest . . ."

"Absolutely not. Why, even if it didn't violate my moral code, the fact is that I know next to nothing about sex. You see, I've always preferred more intellectual pursuits. As a matter of fact, I've never even—but that's another story, and I'd rather not go into it. Suffice it to say that in a wager of the sort you suggest, I'd be a complete novice. Despite the odds of five to one, you'd be in a position to take merciless advantage of me."

"Not really. True, I'm a sex expert. But there's nothing in my background or training that gives me the edge on a

137

novice. Attractiveness is a very subjective thing, and the girl I find most attractive might not necessarily be the girl my opponent finds most attractive. Moreover, neither my opponent nor I can guess which girl each of the men will find most attractive. Consequently, a sexual novice—indeed, even a male virgin—has just as good a chance of winning as the most jaded libertine."

"Do say! Put that way, it makes sense."

"Furthermore," I pressed, "if you decided to bet, it would be up to you to pick the four girls you think will bring their partners to orgasm first. So, even if my expertise gave me an advantage, which it doesn't, I couldn't enjoy the advantage—because you could pick any four girls you chose. I'd have no choice but to cover your bet."

"By Jupiter, you're right! When's the orgy? Not that I plan to attend, you understand, but just for argument's sake, if I *did* decide to attend, when would the orgy be?"

I smiled mischievously. "Are you free tomorrow night?"

"As a matter of fact, I am."

"That's when the orgy is."

He drained his teacup, took out his pouch of tobacco and his package of cigarette papers and nervously rolled himself a smoke. "I must say, Damon, the idea appeals to my instincts as a gambler. Not that I'd attend the orgy, mind you. A man must stick to his principles." He lit the cigarette. "And my principles are, never discuss——"

"You wouldn't be violating your principles," I reminded him. "We wouldn't be discussing sex; we'd merely be betting on it. The circumstances would be identical to those of our bet on the Smythe-Whelan election."

"A valid point, Damon. A valid point. Still, there are other considerations. As you might well imagine, it just wouldn't do to have me walking into an orgy somewhere. Not that I'm concerned with what people would think of me. But, after all, I must think of Lady Brice-Bennington and the Friends of Decency. I couldn't risk blemishing my wife's reputation."

"I could arrange to have the orgy take place right here in your mansion," I interrupted. "Everyone knows that I'm conducting a sex study under the sponsorship of the Friends. Anyone who saw the orgiasts arriving would assume they were merely coming to be interviewed by me."

"True! By Jupiter, it's true! And I really wouldn't be participating in the orgy; I'd just be betting on it! Of course, there's always the matter of how I'd explain things to Lady Brice-Bennington."

"She just said a few minutes ago that she wouldn't mind if you attend the orgy."

"So she did! So she did!" He puffed excitedly on the butt of his cigarette, then ground it out and eagerly rolled another. "What time tomorrow night, Damon? Early, I hope. I like to get to bed before midnight."

"Brice," I promised, grinning wickedly, "you'll be in bed long before midnight."

He chuckled. "And maybe—heh-heh—I'll take a small fortune to bed with me." He patted me fraternally on the shoulder. "Go for broke, Damon. That's what I always say. Gad, does gambling excite me! Gad!!!"

I spent another half-hour with him, drinking tea and smoking a few of his hand-rolled cigarettes. Then I excused myself and headed back to the Eros—but not, of course, before I tipped off Lady B-B and Robbi Randall about what was coming up.

Crew Cut was on duty in the Eros lobby when I got there. Studiously ignoring him, I went up to my room and phoned Peter Blaine. I reported that Diane was safely on her way to the States. Then I asked how he had done with the orgy girls. All five, he replied, were ready and waiting. I told him to have them show up at the Brice-Bennington mansion the following evening at seven. I also told him that he could expect his three bodyguards to arrive at his hideaway sometime during the night. Then, urging him to keep a stiff upper lip, I hung up.

My wristwatch read seven fifteen. I was hungry enough to eat a horse—success always whets my appetite—but I didn't want to leave the hotel because I knew that The Coxe Foundation's dozen men would be calling on me very shortly. So I phoned room service and ordered a steak with all the trimmings. Then I lay back on my bed and, in a move which Lord B-B certainly would applaud, made a little bet with myself as to what would arrive soonest—the steak or the first of the Coxemen.

The bet ended in a draw; the steak and the first Coxeman arrived at exactly the same time. The second Coxeman showed up a few minutes later, and the third arrived just as I was finishing my meal. I told the three of them precisely what I wanted them to do, then dismissed them.

Four more Coxemen came within the hour. I gave them

139

other instructions, then sent them on their way. They were followed by two others, then three more—all of whom were likewise instructed and dismissed.

The dozen men having now been dispatched, I poured myself a stiff Johnnie Walker Black. Then, sitting in my armchair looking out the window, I sipped it. For the first time since I landed in London, I was able to drink with pleasure.

As I sat in my room getting very comfortably high, the Communists undoubtedly were going nuts. The Commie who was on stake-out duty in the lobby couldn't have helped but notice the parade of men coming up to my room. He undoubtedly had informed his headquarters of the development and had been told to tail the first man that left. Meanwhile, the Commie high command had undoubtedly sent more tails into action, so that each of the subsequent Coxeman who left me also could be followed.

Now all twelve Coxemen were galavanting around London, accompanied by a Commie tail—if the Commies had that many men capable of being pressed into service on such short notice. The first three Coxemen had been instructed to shake their tails, then hurry to Peter Blaine's hideout to serve as bodyguards. The others had been told to lead their tails on a wild goose chase all over town.

The game would continue until seven the following evening, when all the Coxeman, along with Peter Blaine and me, had been tailed to the Brice-Bennington mansion. Then it would be time for the tables to turn: The Coxemen would slip out of the mansion, pull guns on their tails, take the tails prisoners and bring them inside.

After that the whole show would be mine—and what a show it would be! I was happily contemplating the grand finale when I heard a knock on my door. I opened it, only to be greeted by a familiar face—a face weatherbeaten and wan, punctuated by a pair of beagle-sad eyes and decorated with a long, walrus-like moustache.

"Damon," said my Coxeman-in-chief, "I don't know what you're up to, but it better be good."

"Sit down," I said, grinning and pouring him a drink. "I'll tell you all about it."

CHAPTER TEN

The blonde was big, beautiful and built like a brick outhouse.

She was followed by a petite brunette, small, svelte and supersexy.

Next came a Chinese girl, with waist-length black hair and a pair of breasts as fantastically firm as they were royally round.

Then came a redhead, a bit small in the breast department, but pure dynamite everywhere else.

Finally, a raven-haired lovely, tall, leggy and oh-so-lithe.

No doubt about it, Peter Blaine knew how to dig them up. There wasn't one girl in the group who couldn't hold her own in a beauty contest—and all four were certified swingers.

Sitting between Walrus-moustache and me on the couch in the Friends of Decency erotic library, Lord B-B watched them undress and tried hard to keep his cool.

"Quite a selection, Damon," he confessed. "It's not easy to pick one's favorite." He added quickly, "Not that I'm excited by any of this, you understand. But, of course, one must recognize attractiveness when one is confronted by it—especially in the nude."

"One must," I agreed, gesturing to the girls to parade back and forth in front of us. "One would be a hypocrite not to."

The girls, one by one, approached our couch, displayed their charms, then backed away.

"I like the redhead myself," observed Walrus-moustache dryly. "Not that I'm trying to influence your bet, Brice."

"I like the redhead too," Lord B-B admitted. "But I also like the blonde. And the Chinese girl is attractive also. As are the brunette and the girl with the black hair. Frankly, Damon, I like them all." Blushing, he added, "Not in a lascivious sense, of course. I'm speaking strictly from an esthetic point of view."

"I understand," I grinned. "As for myself, I like them both esthetically and lasciviously. But, of course, I don't plan to let my carnal appetites run away with me. As I see it, the difference between humans and animals is that humans control their passions and animals don't."

"Well put, Damon," said Lord B-B. "Well put."

Walrus-moustache leered wickedly. "I don't know about you two stoic bastards, but I'd like to throw a good stiff jump into any one of them—and I just might." He elbowed Lord B-B in the ribs for emphasis.

Lord B-B blanched.

"To each his own," I observed superiorly. "To each his own." At the same time I motioned the girls to give us another close look.

They did.

A very close look.

The blonde, who led the parade, brought her enormous breasts within a hair's-breadth of Lord B-B's nose, then inhaled deeply. Lord B-B backed away as though afraid he was going to be singed.

"Inspect the merchandise, Brice," encouraged Walrus-moustache. "How can you tell which one is going to be the most arousing if you don't let them arouse you?"

"I don't get aroused," said Lord B-B, his face ashen. He nervously searched his pockets for his tobacco pouch and his package of cigarette papers.

"Smoke, Brice?" I beamed, tugging a pouch from my pockets. "It's my favorite blend, the one I told you about. My new shipment just arrived today from the States."

"Do say! Love to sample it," he replied, ducking away from the blonde, who was pressing closer to him all the time. "Really, child," he told her, quite unnerved, "I'm not near-sighted! Keep your distance, please!"

Walrus-moustache wedged his hand between her legs. "Don't mind the old geezer, sweetie," he cackled, pulling her toward him. "I'll give you all the loving you need." Whereupon he buried his face between her breasts and began licking at them furiously.

"Sir," hissed Lord B-B, "you're a lout!" Hands trembling, he shook some of my tobacco into his cigarette paper. "Damon," he whispered under his breath, "I don't like your friend at all."

"Ignore him, Brice," I smiled. "He just envies your self-control."

The blonde having moved aside, the petite brunette ap-

142

proached Lord B-B. Cupping her breasts in her hands, she lifted them toward him. At the same time her svelte little hips moved in a slow, gyrating motion.

"I've always wanted to make love to a Lord," she purred. "I think it'd be so exciting."

Lord B-B winced. "A match, Damon," he said, leaning away from her. "Quickly, a match!"

I lit his cigarette. Walrus-moustache shoved the blonde aside and began fondling the brunette.

"Dirty old man," observed Lord B-B. He inhaled deeply. "Strange aroma to this tobacco, Damon. A bit pungent, wouldn't you say?" He looked off into the distance. "Goes down rather harshly too. Not nearly as mild as mine."

I grinned. "Give it a chance, Brice. Take a few more drags and see if you don't like it better."

The Chinese girl replaced the brunette. The model of discretion, she kept a full two paces away from Lord B-B, but the feline movements of her body were sexy in the extreme, and even more disconcerting to him than the aggressiveness of the blonde and the brunette.

"A regular temptress, that one," Lord B-B admitted, taking another puff of dynamite hash. "A regular Salome!"

"She's getting a rise out of you, huh?" grinned Walrus-moustache, giving our host another elbow in the ribs. "Glad to see it! Glad to see it!"

"Oh, for Pete's sake, shut up!" said Lord B-B, Puffing nervously on the cigarette, he said to me, "A total boor, this man. A total boor."

"Try holding the smoke in your lungs as long as you can, Brice," I smiled. "That takes the harshness away."

The redhead took her turn in front of Lord B-B. She dropped to her knees, keeping them spread widely apart. Then she leaned back until her head was almost touching her heels. Her pert, small breasts quivered like two scoops of jello. Her hips, at the same time, undulated provocatively.

"Ahhhhh, what a spectacle," sighed Walrus-moustache. "And to think some people prefer the opera!"

Lord B-B looked at her appreciatingly. "Lovely body," he mused. "And she moves it so excitingly." Suddenly he stiffened. "What am I saying? What on earth am I saying?" He closed his eyes, as if to shut out the impulses that appeared to be taking possession of him, and took another deep drag on the cigarette.

143

The redhead moved aside, and the raven-haired beauty did her turn. Twirling her body, she offered our host a fantastic panorama of curves and delicious crevasses.

Lord B-B opened his eyes and smiled dreamily. "Beautiful girl," he purred. "Beautiful girl. And such marvelous tobacco, Damon. It tastes so good. And it smells so good."

"Take another drag," I prodded him. "It gets better all the time."

Walrus-moustache, scampering onto the floor and licking the girl's navel as his hands closed around her hips and pressed her pubes against him, saying "It's not how long you make it, it's how long you make it last, la la, la la, la la."

I waited until my Coxeman-in-chief had finished doing his thing. Then I nudged Lord B-B. "Well, Brice," I said, "you've seen the girls now. Would you like another look, or are you ready to place your bet?"

He seemed to ponder the idea, then, taking another deep drag of Peter Blaine's hash, said, "Let's bet, Damon." Pause. "No, let's give the girls another look." Pause. "No, let's bet." Pause. "Oh, I don't care what we do, it's all so much fun!"

Walrus-moustache tossed me a sideways glance. "If that grass ain't Panamanian Purple," he smirked, "it's the next best thing."

It sure as hell was! And it was working a lot faster than I had dreamed it would. If I didn't get the show on the road fast, old Lord B-B would be too stoned to do what I wanted him to do when the time came for it.

"Let's bet," I said quickly. "You've seen all the girls. Now, what's your choice for the first four?"

His face took on a studious look as he scrutinized them, all standing in line facing us. For a moment he said nothing; he just beamed at them appreciatingly. Then, chuckling to himself, he said, "I'll parlay a thousand pounds. The girl with the black hair is number one."

Walrus-moustache grimaced. He knew his arithmetic. The taxpayers would hate us one and a half million dollars worth if Lord B-B won—even if they didn't know we existed.

I gulped. "Okay, who's number two?"

He waited all of half a minute before answering. "The redhead."

"And number three?"

He took a deep drag on the cigarette then stared dreamily into space.

"Number three?" Walrus-moustache echoed.

"The brunette." Pause. "No, the blonde." Pause. "Oh, who cares?"

"Pick one," I insisted.

"The brunette," he giggled. "Why the hell not!"

"And number four?" asked Walrus-moustache.

Lord B-B waited a full minute before answering. "I like—I like—"

"Yes? Yes?"

"I like New York in June, how about you?" he sang.

"If there's anything I can't stand," muttered Walrus-moustache, "it's a prig that can't hold his pot."

"Number four," I prompted. "The Chinese girl or the blonde?"

"Oh hell, the Chinese girl," he laughed. "No discrimination here, nossir!" He took another drag on the joint. Fortunately, by this time it had burned down to his fingers. He dropped it into an ashtray. I hated to think what shape he'd've been in if it had been a silly millimeter longer.

The bets having been placed and recorded, I gestured to the girls. They promptly positioned themselves on their backs on the mattresses which had been set up in the middle of the room for precisely this purpose. Walrus-moustache then went to the door of the room where five of our Coxeman were waiting, rapped sharply, opened the door, and yelled, "Okay, fellas, go get 'em!"

The Coxemen dashed into the room like horses racing out of their starting gate. The first leaped onto the redhead, who welcomed him with open legs. The second took the Chinese girl. The third and fourth fought over the blonde; then the third won, and the fourth scampered over to the brunette's mattress. The raven-haired beauty had already been claimed by the fifth.

The race was on. I watched bemusedly, as did Walrus-moustache. But Lord B-B was on the edge of his seat, cheering like a madman. "Come on, Blackie!" he called to the raven-haired swinger. "Move those hips! Let him have it! Sock it to him!"

And she did. Her partner pumped away atop her like a piston for thirty or forty seconds. Then, grinning triumphantly, he sprung to his feet.

"The winnah!" cried Walrus-moustache.

"You owe me five thousand pounds, Damon," said Lord B-B, seeming very sober all of a sudden.

"It's a parlay," I smiled. "Three more contests to go."

145

The guy with the redhead promptly swung into high gear. I sensed his climax even before he vacated the saddle.

"Two in a row!" said Walrus-moustache.

"Five times five is twenty-five thousand," said Lord B-B. Turning to the contestants again, he cheered, "Come on, brunette! Sock it to him! Sock it to him!"

"Brunette!" groaned Walrus-moustache as her partner drove home the final thrust, then stood up. Evidently my Coxeman-in-chief had suddenly become very worried about my money. And with good reason. My money was his money.

"Twenty-five times five is a hundred and twenty-five thousand pounds," said Lord B-B. "Go, China-girl! Baby needs a new pair of shoes! Seven comes eleven! Sock it to him!"

She socked.

But fortunately for The Coxe Foundation's coffers, the blonde socked a little harder—and her partner got there a little sooner.

"The blonde!" cheered Walrus-moustache, his face testifying to his relief.

"Damn!" hissed Lord B-B.

"You can't win 'em all," I smiled glibly.

"Up yours," he riposted.

Walrus-moustache threw a fraternal arm around our host's shoulders. "Cheer up, Brice. Have another one of Damon's cigarettes. Then I'll give you a chance to get your money back."

Lord B-B's expression brightened. "Another parlay?"

Walrus-moustache grinned. "Not quite. A side bet, double or nothing, my thousand pounds against the thousand you lost and a thousand more."

Lord B-B's scowl made it clear that he didn't like the odds. But, as he had said so many times, he was a gambling man; he had just tossed a thousand down the drain, and he couldn't stand to see them go without putting up a fight. "What's the contest?" he asked.

Walrus-moustache surveyed the five girls, who still were lying on their mattresses. "This girl with the black hair," he said, appearing to be lost in serious thought, "has proved herself beyond a doubt to be the champion of the group. But who's to say which mode of love-making she's most efficient in? Some girls are best at doing what comes naturally, while others are more proficient at what, for lack of a more delicate term, I'll refer to as back-door love-making."

"You mean—?"

146

"Precisely. Buggery, Brice. Buggery. Now, what I propose is this: Friend Damon here has always been a front-door suitor, and I, by fortunate coincidence, have always been a back-door lover. So what do you say the the both of us make love to her at the same time—Damon from the front, me from the rear! You decide which one of us will cimax first. If you're right, you lose nothing. If you're wrong, you owe Damon the thousand you orignally lost to him and you owe me a thousand more."

"That's not a very sporting proposition," said Lord B-B sourly.

Walrus-moustache shrugged. "If you like, we can always call it quits right now. Pay Damon the thousand pounds and we'll all be on our way."

I waited with bated breath for the answer. If The Big Prig decided to call it quits then and there, I'd've lost my shot at the caper I was really counting on.

Lord B-B scowled. "Give me a cigarette, Damon," he said.

"By all means, Brice." I proferred my pouch. "By all means."

He slowly rolled another joint. Then, after lighting it and taking a deep drag, he said, "Okay, it's a bet. And I'm betting on Damon."

I sighed my relief. Walrus-moustache merely smiled. We both undressed.

The raven-haired beauty joined us on the mattress closest to the couch where Lord B-B was still sitting. I lay on my back, and she lay alongside me, maneuvering one thigh over my hips. I deftly maneuvered my ship into port. Then she rolled onto her side, and as I rolled with her, Walrus-moustache established his connection.

"On three," said my Coxeman-in-chief, whose talent for libertinage, heretofore undisplayed, I found quite surprising. "One . . . two . . . three . . . GO!!!"

We went. Lord B-B, dragging heavily on his second stick of hash in less than half an hour, cried, "Work out, Damon! Go to it! Give it all you've got!"

I pumped away furiously. The reciprocal motions of Walrus-moustache doing his own thing made my work all the easier. And the raven-haired beauty made it easier still.

She was nothing short of sensational. Every part of her erogenous zones were alive with passion. And the rest of her body wasn't exactly out of the picture either. She couldn't press her breasts against me because Walrus-moustache had his hands around them, but she licked at my face and neck with her tongue, and her teeth nibbled teasingly and excitingly at my flesh.

"Go, Damon, go!" called Lord B-B, getting higher all the time. "I'm counting on you! Don't let me down, boy!"

I was so impressed by his loyalty that I almost wanted him to win. Almost, but not quite. I knew that my only hope for setting up The Big Caper—the caper that would put an end forever to the Friends of Decency—lay in getting The Coxe Foundation's hooks even more deeply imbedded into his bankroll.

I paced myself. Though I continued to move like a dynamo, I forced myself to think non-sexy thoughts. I also bit my lip and concentrated on the pain—that favorite trick of mine to delay the onset of the inevitable.

On the other side of the raven-haired beauty, Walrus-moustache was thrusting away to beat the band. His thrusts made her thrust harder, and her thrusts sent wild shock waves of sensation through me. Try though I might, I knew I couldn't hold out much longer.

And I didn't.

Maybe it was all the tension I had experienced during the past few days.

Mabye it was just the excitement of playing the orgy game after so long a period of nothing but one-to-one sex.

Whatever it was, I very rapidly found myself on the edge of the ledge.

And once on the edge, I plunged into orgasm's abyss—deeply, fully, totally.

It was at that point that I did something no genuine gambler's gambler would ever do: I cheated.

But, of course, I wasn't a genuine gambler's gambler. I had only been playing the role for Lord B-B's benefit. At heart I was just a sex-happy young sociologist with a mission to perform for The Coxe Foundation—a mission one aspect of which involved the dissolution of the Friends of Decency.

So I cheated. Even though I had climaxed, I stayed in the saddle and—thanks to my insatiable virility—continued to pump away. My duplicity was costing Lord B-B two thousand pounds. But there was no way he could know I was cheating him! My perpetual erection assured that!

"Come on, Damon! Come on, boy!" my eager cheerleader was shouting. "Sock it to her! Sock it to her!"

148

I socked it to her.

And so did Walrus-moustache.

A minute passed, then another. My back was beginning to ache, and my legs were getting very tired. But I held on. Painful though it was, I held on.

And then I didn't have to hold on any longer.

"The winnah!" exulted Walrus-moustache, springing to his feet and clasping his hands over his head. His fallen soldier was proof of his triumph. "That's two thousand pounds, Brice. Would you like to try for four?"

Lord B-B was nonplussed. "Two thousand pounds," he giggled. Then, taking a very deep drag on his cigarette, which had been smoked down to almost nothing, he smiled ecstatically and said: "What's two thousand pounds?"

I got up from the mattress. "Brice," I said smiling, "I'm going to give you one more chance to get even. And I'm going to offer you odds you can't resist. Your investment will be a single pound—just one pound, Brice. And mine will be the two thousand you lost so far. If you win, you get your two thousand back. If I win, you pay out two thousand and one."

He looked at me through glazed eyes. "What's the contest?"

"Have another cigarette," I said, offering him my pouch. "Then I'll tell you all about it."

He obediently rolled a new joint and lit it.

"Brice," I said, "there's a rumor going around that you've got fantastic will power when it comes to sex. According to what I hear, there isn't a woman alive that can get you excited. But I think I know a woman who can. Now here's the bet: You're going to spend an hour in bed with this woman. One hour. During that time, neither one of you can speak a word. But she's going to use every nonverbal means at her command to arouse you. If she succeeds—if she gets you excited enough that you make love to her—I win the bet. If she fails, you win the bet. I'm confident enough in her abilities that I'm offering you odds of two thousand to one."

He looked thoughtfully at his freshly lit joint. "Excellent tobacco here, Damon. Excellent. Moroccan, you say? I must get the name of your tobacconist. Delightful smoke. Harsh at first, but very mild now. Quite wonderful, really."

"The bet, Brice," I reminded him. "What do you say?"

He chuckled, as if I had to be a fool to ask. "At odds of two thousand to one? Of course I'll take it, Damon. Bring on

149

your wonder woman! I'll show her what resistance really is!"

I went to the adjacent room, returning a few seconds later with Robbi Randall, who had been standing by just waiting for the word to spring into action. She had abandoned the severe tweeds that were her usual costume around the Friends of Decency in favor of a see-through outfit very similar to the one she had worn the night she came calling at the laboratory of the League for Sexual Dynamics. What I saw through Robbi's see-through was enough to set my pulse racing—even though I had just gone a very vigorous round with the raven-haired beauty.

"Miss Randall!" exclaimed Lord B-B, taken aback. "My word! You're practically naked!"

"All the better to turn you on, milord," she purred, playing the seductress role to the hilt. "Wouldn't you like to go to bed with me?"

"Gad, would I!" he gasped. Then, as an aside, he added, "But what would Lady Brice-Bennington say?"

"She said," I reminded him, "that you had her permission to attend the orgy. And, in any case, she'll never find out. Robbi is leaving with me for the States in just a few hours."

A man in full possession of his faculties probably would have required a more detailed explanation. But Lord B-B, under control of Muse Mary Jane, seemed perfectly content.

"Brice, baby," cooed Robbi, throwing one arm around his shoulders and reaching with the other for his crotch, "what do you say we try making beautiful music together?"

He reached hesitatingly for her breast, then, in a sudden burst of enthusiasm, clutched it vigorously through her see-through. "Ahhhhhhh!!!" he sighed. "Gad, that feels good!" Turning to me, he said: "Damon, I think I'm going to lose the bet." Then, beaming happily, he added: "But what the hell's one pound more or less?"

"The lovers," I told Walrus-moustache, "should be left alone. I've got a canopied bed set up in the next room and they can do their stuff in there whenever they're ready. Meanwhile, let's let them warm up to the occasion with a little foreplay out here."

"Whatever you say, Damon," he replied obligingly. "Actually, I was getting a little bored with all this anyway. We've got a few gentlemen down in the cellar that I'd like to talk to. And I've a few questions to ask you once we're finished with them."

"Then let's be off, shall we?" I gestured toward the door leading to the cellar stairs.

Down in the cellar, a baker's dozen of Communist agents were seated Indian-chief-style on the floor. Their wrists were bound behind their backs, and their faces wore expressions of acute displeasure. Guarding them were the seven of our Coxemen who hadn't been pressed into service for the orgy.

Rounding up the Commies had been a cinch. After taking them on a wild goose chase for twenty-four hours, the Coxemen had simply led them to the mansion. Then, while all the tails were waiting outside to see what would happen next, the Coxeman had done a turnabout and, with guns, had taken the tails prisoner. Now they were all here—Rumpled Suit, Mod Type, Crew Cut, an assortment of flunkies whom I'd yet to nickname, and, in the middle of the circle, the big man behind the operation, Michaelson, the gent with the monocle who had been my tablemate that first evening at The Safari Club.

"Gentlemen," I told them, as Walrus-moustache and I joined the group, "you've got two alternatives: either defect to the West and work for our side from now on, or take your chances with the boys back home. You realize, of course, that if you select the latter alternative, it's Siberia for all of you."

Michaelson scowled. "You're bluffing, Damon. You don't have anything on us, and you know it."

I grinned sarcastically. "Don't I? Well, let's see."

Walrus-moustache promptly disappeared into an adjacent room and reappeared moments later with Peter Blaine. The erstwhile pimp looked more relaxed than I had ever seen him.

"Take a look at these pictures, Michaelson," said Walrus-moustache, displaying the prints of the Commie agents and their girlfriends which I had taken from Blaine's safe deposit box. "Here's proof that you and your boys were lying down on the job—or should I say *laying* down on the job? While you should've been spying you were playing games. Blaine caught you in the act. He didn't know how to get you in trouble with these pictures, because he doesn't know who your boss is. But I do know who your boss is— and I know how he feels about agents who lose sight of their mission and get involved in extracurricular affairs. I also happen to know of a Russian spy in Rangoon who just hates Rangoon and who'd like nothing more than to move into your job here in

151

England. All I've got to do is see to it that this fellow gets these photographs. You'll be on the next *Aeroflot* back to Moscow before you can say Tovarrich Robinson."

"But," protested Michaelson, "we made love to the girls only in the line of duty. We were working on a case."

"Try explaining that to your boss," grinned Walrus-moustache. "He'll want to know what case you were working on. And, when you tell him the Smythe-Whelan case, you'll find that you don't have a case at all."

"We do have a case," said Michaelson. "We have photos of Smythe and Whelan with their girlfriends—in very compromising positions."

"The photos are meaningless," I said. "If you used them when you first got them, you might've set off a scandal that could've toppled Prime Minister Wilson's regime. But you didn't. And now you can't. It's too late. The photos are useless without the girls who appear in them. One of the girls, Andi Gleason, is dead. The other girl, Diane Dionne, is in the United States. Without witnesses to back up the photos, you really don't have a case. If you turned the photos over to the newspapers, they'd think you doctored them to help Smythe and Whelan's opponents. If you turned them over to your bosses, they'd think you doctored them to save your own neck."

"You made your big mistake, Michaelson," continued Walrus-moustache, "when you shot for the big prize. You thought there was one. But there wasn't. That error of judgment proved to be your downfall."

"And it really was one hell of an error of judgment," I put in. "This whole fiasco got started when Peter Blaine and his girlfriends decided to try shaking down Smythe and Whelan for cash. Blaine arranged to get Smythe and Whelan involved in affairs with his girls. He originally planned to get just enough evidence on Smythe and Whelan so that he could sell his girls' stories to the newspapers. But, while he was getting his evidence, he learned that a certain guy named Christopher Smythe—the M.P.'s namesake, but definitely not the M.P.—had inherited a twenty-four-million-dollar fortune. Blaine didn't realize that the guy was just a namesake; he thought that M.P. Christopher Blaine had inherited the money, and he tired to shake him down for it."

"The M.P.," Walrus-moustache went on, "didn't have the money, so he couldn't pay Blaine off. Meanwhile, a number of other people had gotten wind of the Smythe-Whelan affair."

"The Friends of Decency got wind of it," I said, "and they made a feeble attempt at finding out what was what. But, of course, they weren't really equipped to do the kind of work we spy people do, so, after fishing around for a while trying to get evidence, they backed off. It wasn't that they disbelieved the rumors they had heard. It was just that they saw no point in rowing upstream when they didn't have to. And they didn't have to. I wasn't aware of it until just recently, but the Friends had all the reason in the world to believe that Smythe and Whelan wouldn't get back into office. The districts which Smythe and Whelan represented in Parliament are staunch religious districts. Smythe and Whelan had aroused the antagonism of the clergymen in these districts by taking a firm stand against censorship of erotic literature and films. When it later was revealed that both Smythe and Whelan held stock in an American publisher of erotic books, Smythe and Whelan were as good as out of office." To Walrus-moustache, and almost as an aside, I added, "One of the things I hadn't been able to figure out about this case was why Lord Brice-Bennington had been confident that Smythe and Whelan would lose—so confident that he was willing to bet me five hundred pounds that not just one but both of them would. The reason he was so confident was because he had been alert to the reaction of the constituents in these districts to the holding by Smythe and Whelan of the American publishing stocks."

"So," said Walrus-moustache, "the Friends of Decency had investigated the possible connection between Smythe and Whelan and their girlfriends, but had lost interest in the matter after a very short while. Meanwhile, The Coxe Foundation had also investigated, and our agents had, on their own, gotten the same evidence that Peter Blaine had."

"But," I added triumphantly, "your people, Michaelson, hadn't gotten this same evidence. So you continued to tail Blaine and his girlfriends, hoping that you'd eventually come across what you wanted. All you wanted at the time was evidence that you could use to throw the election to Smythe and Whelan's opponents. Then I showed up on the scene and you guessed that there might be something bigger at stake."

"Yes," said Walrus-moustache. "Damon's arrival in London to conduct a sex study under the auspices of the Friends of Decency was publicized. Your bosses back in the Kremlin learned of it as a matter of course, and they became suspicious."

"They became suspicious," I said, "because this wasn't the first time one of my highly publicized studies coincided with an affair you people were interested in. I've worked many times when your people worked with me hand-in-hand. By this time, I'd become a very familiar face to Russia's international spy headquarters. My government had been using me too heavily on too many cases, and my undercover value had diminished considerably."

"But," continued Walrus-moustache, "in this case your recognition of Damon worked to our advantage. This time, you see, he wasn't working on a case for us. He had come to London to conduct a bona fide sex study. However, because you people knew about the Smythe-Whelan caper that Blaine was working on, you automatically assumed that we knew —and you assumed when Damon's sex study was publicized that we were sending him here to work on the same case."

"Which really wasn't true," I lied. "But, of course, you didn't know it wasn't true. So you had me tailed from the moment I arrived in London. And when I showed up at The Safari Club, you were positive I had been sent here to work on the case. Actually I had gone to The Safari Club just by coincidence. I wanted a night on the town, and a little sex action. You personally picked up on me at The Safari Club, Michaelson, and, when you saw me move in on Andi Gleason, you were even more positive that you and I were both after the same thing—something to do with the Smythe-Whelan affair."

"That's why," said Walrus-moustache, "you really stepped up your program. Until Damon arrived, you were content to take your good-natured time trying to get evidence on Smythe and Whelan. But once you saw him on the scene—and making a play for Andi Gleason, yet—you assumed that there must be something more involved than just the threat of a scandal. You were wrong, of course, but you didn't know you were wrong, so you pulled out all the stops. You approached Peter Blaine and tried to force him to play ball with you. And when that failed, you broke into his apartment, and, since he had been foolish enough to leave photos of Smythe and Whelan and the girls lying around, you got the evidence you wanted."

"But then," I said, "you were afraid to use the evidence. You figured that I was after something more than you were, and you didn't know what. So you made a bold move. Without even knowing what you were looking for, you approached Christopher Smythe and tried to get him to tell you what it was you thought he was trying to hide."

"Smythe," Walrus-moustache went on, "was a weakling in many ways. In addition to serving as his lover, Andi Gleason had been his supplier of drugs, to which she had introduced him during the course of their affair. He was then dependent on drugs, and he was dependent on Andi to supply them. James Whelan was equally dependent on Diane Dionne. That's why when the American spy network approached them through diplomatic channels and asked them to kiss their girlfriends goodbye, they refused. They needed their drugs, and the girls were the only people whom they knew they could count on to supply them."

"But," I said pointedly, "while Smythe and Whelan were weak when it came to drugs, they were strong when it came to national loyalty. They wouldn't sell out to you people, Michaelson, if their lives depended on it. And when you, panicked by my appearance on the scene, put pressure on Smythe, he made sure that you couldn't possibly put his loyalty to a test. He made sure by killing himself."

"Your strong-arm tactics," said Walrus-moustache, "really blew that attempt for you, Michaelson. That's one thing you Commies can't understand—national loyalty. Your government keeps you loyal by putting a gun in your back. Democratic governments inspire loyalty rather than threaten it. Smythe was loyal, and he killed himself rather than let you high-pressure him into doing your bidding once he got back into office."

"After Smythe was killed," I continued, "you backed off on Whelan. You didn't want to risk losing the only other prospective turncoat you had. And, because I was on the scene, you were sure Whelan was another turncoat. You were, of course, wrong."

"Meanwhile," said Walrus-moustache, "Damon couldn't help noticing how your people had been tailing him all over the city. He wondered why you were tailing him and he connected it with his rendezvous with Andi Gleason."

"I followed up on Andi," I went on, "and she led me to Blaine, who told me about how you were trying to muscle in on his caper. That's when I contacted my boss and let him know that I'd accidentally happened on a spy caper that he'd be interested in."

"The rest," said Walrus-moustache, "is ancient history. We sent a group of men to Damon's room and your people tailed them. Then we did a turnaround on your tails, and here you sit. Now, what will it be? Do you defect to the West, or do we see to it that all of you get shipped off to Siberia?"

Michaelson shook his head sadly. "I should've been an accountant," he murmured. "When I was a boy, I used to love mathematics and everything that had to do with figures. I could've been very happy in Kiev, tending to the books of our communal stores. But no, I had to look for adventure and excitement as a spy! How stupid!"

Walrus-moustache smiled. "Win some, lose some. And you just lost the big one." He turned to one of his Coxemen. "Give these gentlemen another fifteen minutes to weigh their decision. Then I'll be back to talk business with them. Meanwhile, Damon and I have to check up on the progress of a wager that's being decided upstairs."

We headed toward the room where the orgy had been staged. Peter Blaine accompanied us.

"Boy," he said on the way up the cellar stairs, "you guys really know your business."

"That's part of being a pro," smiled Walrus-moustache. "The pros know their business. The amateurs don't."

"What I can't understand, though," said Blaine, "is why the Communists killed Andi. I mean, you guys said that the photos of Smythe and Whelan with the girls would be useless without the girls' testimony. If the Commies needed the girls' testimony, whey did they kill one of the girls?"

"They didn't," I said.

"Then who killed Andi?"

"She died accidentally just like it said in the police report. I couldn't understand it myself when it happened. I couldn't believe that a girl who was in full possession of her faculties would simply walk out into traffic and get run down—especially when she was involved in a case like this one. It seemed like too much to ask of coincidence. But then I saw Diane walk into a doorframe at the apartment where you and I met yesterday, and everything became clear to me. What I had forgotten when I discounted coincidence was that Andi wasn't a girl in full possession of her faculties. Like Diane, she was a dyed-in-the-wood pothead. She was zonked out of her mind the night I made love to her. And I'd bet my bottom dollar that she stayed zonked, because she was scared stiff of the

156

Communists and of everything else that was happening. The more scared she got, the more zonked she got. And finally she was so zonked that she just stepped out in front of a car. The driver who killed her probably didn't stop because he was afraid of criminal charges. Hit-and-run accidents happen all the time."

"Then—then—" Blaine stammered, "if the Communists didn't kill her, they probably wouldn't have killed me or Diane either. You were bluffing, Damon! You fooled me!"

"That's part of being a pro, Blaine," I grinned, echoing Walrus-moustache. "The pros know their business, and the amateurs don't."

We reached the room where the orgy had taken place. Blaine's five girls had been dismissed for the night, and the five Coxemen who had been their sex partners were all sitting around trying their best to inspire the interest of the sexy blonde in the see-through blouse who was sitting on the couch regarding them with an expression of total indifference. The blonde was Robbi Randall.

"What's this?" gasped Walrus-moustache. "The hour isn't up yet. Where's Lord Brice-Bennington?"

I slid into place on the couch next to Robbi. My hand found the succulent expanse of bare thigh beneath the hem of her mini, and I stroked the flesh lovingly. Now that she no longer had to play the method-role, she responded by pressing sexily against me.

"Lord Brice-Bennington, heretofore called another Big Prig," I smiled, "is presently in the process of getting his rocks off—for the first time, believe it or not, in his forty-odd years."

"Not the first time," Robbi corrected me, sliding five delicate fingers up my leg. "I've been keeping count, and, as of now, he's working on his third time."

"But," asked Walrus-moustache, eyes wide, "you're out here! What is he, some kind of solo-sexual?"

"No," I chuckled, "he has a partner."

"Well for Pete's sake, whom?"

My chuckle blossomed into a full-blown laugh. "You'll find out in a few minutes—just as soon, in fact, as he finishes his third round."

"And that won't be long," put in Robbi, nibbling on my ear. "Just listen to him!"

We listened. Lord B-B's bed was in the next room, and the

157

door was open. The springs of the bed were squeaking to beat the band. Lord B-B was saying, "By Gad! Who'd ever believe it!? Ah, Robbi darling, it's sensational! I can't wait to tell Penelope!"

"Damon," said Walrus-moustache, "I demand an explanation."

"You'll get one," I supplied. "When I turned Lady B-B on to the pleasures of sex, I wondered how I might turn Lord B-B on also. I thought of moral suasion, but I remembered that he had that inflexible principle which guides his life—he absolutely refused to discuss four subjects: politics, sex, religion and literature. The mention of literature brought to mind a very famous work of English literature, Chaucer's *Canterbury Tales*, and more specifically, one of these tales, 'The Miller's Tale.' "

"You mean—?" said Walrus-moustache, suddenly realizing what was up.

But I was too involved with Robbi Randall to answer immediately. My tongue was in her mouth and my fingers had found their way up her marvelous thigh and into the super-sweet warmth of her splendid honey pot. What was better yet, she hadn't needed a method-director to tell her how to respond!

"Ahhhhhhhhhh!!!" came Lord B-B's cry from the next room. "Ahhhhhh!!!" Then, a moment later: "Well, so much for the Friends of Decency. As of now, Robbi dearest, I'm off the wagon. And I'm going forthwith to Lady B-B's chamber. There's still some lead left in the old pencil, and she's going to get her share!"

"She got her share," came a soft female voice in reply. "And she loved every minute of it, darling."

"What's that!" shouted Lord B-B. "Penelope—can I believe my ears?"

"You can, dearest," she sighed ecstatically. "You can!"

"But of course!" said Walrus-moustache. "The Miller's Tale. A man is enticed into the bed of a woman he believes to be a harlot. The room is dark and he can't see her. They make love and he suddenly discovers that he's just made love to his own wife. That's it, Damon, isn't it? That's it!"

"Ah, Penelope!" sighed Lord B-B. "To think of all the time we've wasted."

"Forget the time we wasted, darling," said she. "Think of the times ahead. Forget your silly repressions. Remember, it's what's up front that counts."

"Damon," said Walrus-moustache, "answer me! Do I have The Miller's Tale right or not?" Pause. "Damon!" Pause. "Oh, for Pete's sake, Damon, have you no decency at all? Right here? In front of all these people?"

Yep.

Right there in front of all those people.

I would have answered him, but it's pretty hard to talk when your tongue is in the mouth of one of the most beautiful creatures you've ever seen, and her legs are wrapped around you, and her fingernails are digging fiercely into your back, and her hips are pumping a mile a minute, stoking your passions to higher and higher peaks.

Lady B-B had got her share.

And now, with Robbi Randall, I, at last, was getting mine.

What a beautiful way to wrap up an assignment!